Temptation So Sweet

FELICIA JOHNSON

authorHOUSE®

AuthorHouse™
1663 Liberty Drive
Bloomington, IN 47403
www.authorhouse.com
Phone: 1 (800) 839-8640

Published by AuthorHouse   05/14/2015

ISBN: 978-1-5049-0069-0 (sc)
ISBN: 978-1-5049-0068-3 (e)

Library of Congress Control Number: 2015903938

Print information available on the last page.

Any people depicted in stock imagery provided by Thinkstock are models, and such images are being used for illustrative purposes only. Certain stock imagery © Thinkstock.

This book is printed on acid-free paper.

Contents

Prologue

T HIS HAD TO BE the most exhausting day of her life. Pharise Mallard had screwed up royally this time. She had blamed Jason Williams, her boss, of not being objective when he accused her of submitting her worst legal analysis in the last six years. Jason told her that it was vague, elementary, and that she had failed to discover how the company that was being sued was negligent in keeping their employees safe. Sure, Pharise had given him her analysis and she believed it was pretty good at the time. Jason's criticism hurt. So, her mouth started moving before her head processed what he was trying to tell her. As usual she jumped the guns once again. She had torn into Jason accusing him of being biased, unrealistic in his expectations, and verbalized that it was getting more and more difficult to work for him. Pharise used her catalogue of words to annihilate his character, integrity, and his assessment abilities of her evaluation of this case. Jason was hurt, but his poker face showed little expression as she ranted on and on. This was the first time that she had exemplified this type of behavior during a performance review. Up until this point, she had been consistently at the top of her game and enjoyed a six-figure salary as a nurse whose responsibilities included investigating and documenting safety infractions that potentially could result in bodily harm for employees. This was a first for her. Her performance was lacking to say the least. Most of her family member's were over achievers and her name topped the list. Repeatedly, she sought out the most difficult cases, always meeting deadlines with time to spare. If negligence existed, she was the "go to" person to uncover it. She was meticulous to a fault. No stone was ever left unturned and her history included reviewing every policy and procedure manual, the medical records of the injured workers, the working conditions, environmental conditions, reviewing every standard operating procedure, and looking at all of the company's practices. More than this, she had always been able to take Jason's objective criticism. Those comments helped her to achieve her present level of success. And if she were honest with herself, she knew that he was correct in his assessment of her review of the case. The report wasn't thorough, nor had it found anything that they hadn't already known. Maybe, she was a little burned out. Lately, sleep avoided her and her focus was way off.

Allegory Medical was a manufacturing company that produced prosthetics and other medical appliances used for surgical procedures. The word on the street was that the company was notorious for taking short-cuts and placing their employees in harm's way. Their practices were inconsistent and they failed to provide their worker's with a safe environment, but her report had not been able to offer them an edge in defending their clients who were part of a class action suit.

Jason was probably right, she was burned out. If truth be told, she had been that way for the last two years since she lost her mother. Since that time, she had been on auto-pilot. Her friends had even sensed the subtle changes and wondered when they would get their old friend back. She was distant and further alienated them by finding excuses not to attend the all-girl "get togethers". She missed Angel's celebration of her new job, Shandra's son graduation and Adriane's wedding. These were her girls and she still had not wanted to participate in their celebrations. This had to mean something, but she just could not figure out what. She concluded that she just didn't have the energy for all the hoop-la.

Jason suggested she take some time off to get herself together and really figure out what she wanted to do for the next 30 years career-wise. In fact, he insisted that she take a vacation and get a change of scenery. He said it felt like he was losing his best employee. Right now her head hurt, her stomach churned and she hadn't had a good night's sleep in so long that she couldn't even remember. Her doctor had prescribed her one of those anti-depressant drugs that claimed to be able to change one's depressed state. They hadn't helped her, probably because she refused to take anything that might cause her to lose control. Pharise had been taking the prescribed medication that should have helped her sleep, but sleep still eluded her. It could have been because of the nightmares. The nightmares seemed to all have a common theme, that she was lost or being chased. She wondered what that was all about. She had been bothered by stomach problems every since she had become a nurse ten years ago and worked twelve-hour shifts. It was then that she was diagnosed as having "irritable bowel syndrome", which translated into whenever she was stressed her stomach hurt. She knew that her mother would want her to get on with her life. Her mother had invested so much in her and her siblings. Momma had prepared her family well for life's ups and downs. She had been the rock for her family, her school, the community and her church. In fact, she was the glue that held everything together. Somehow, Pharise had gotten stuck and could not move forward. It was too painful to not have her around. These same feelings had seeped into the quality of her work. Jason had been kind in his remarks and she had been brutal in hers. There was no doubt that she would have to apologize to him soon. Maybe, she wouldn't procrastinate and do it today. She had been apologizing a lot lately, to her friends, to her boss, to her co-workers, to the people at the bank, to the people at the store, and so on. She was a lit fuse and her patience had crossed the line for being thin. Things needed to change or she would continue to spiral downward. Obviously, this was what others might call her dark side and she didn't care for it at all.

Chapter 1

THE MORNING STARTED with a promise of something new. She couldn't quite figure out the reason why she had this familiar feeling in her stomach. She was following her bosses' suggestion to take a vacation. Pharise had called Jason to apologize for literally having a break down in his office that day. He accepted her apology easily. Realizing she needed to release the emotions that had been haunting her for the past two years since the day she had left her mother at the hospital for the last time. She would trade anything to go back to that day, but fate would not allow it. Instead, she was off to take the long overdue time to recover and heal. She was headed to Washington, DC, one of her favorite places. Pharise loved the feel of the city and the crisp air. It was late summer and fall was waiting patiently on the horizon. The Renaissance Hotel would be her temporary home, another favorite of hers. It was located downtown in the midst of a cultural Mecca.

Although Jason had suggested she not think about work, an old case that was still open was suddenly on her mind. If she got a chance, she would do a little more background on it to see if anything came up. The last time she was in DC, nothing blatant stood out. However, there was something unsettling about the company and because of the allegations that one of the employees had initiated. She couldn't quite tell if she was just dealing with a disgruntled employee or whether there truly was some merit to the allegations. While taking it easy, she would do a little investigation into the affairs of Allegory Medical and see what she could find out.

The Renaissance hotel was grand to say the least. It was a mixture of contemporary and elegant ambience. One could always find someone famous milling in the lobby or hanging out in the guest area. She was always wide-eyed when she saw a movie star or television icon. This was indeed the place to be. She stood at the hotel registration counter lost in her own thoughts when the registration clerk asked for the third time, "may I help you". Quickly recovering, Pharise offered her name. Jason's secretary had actually made her travel arrangement. She opened the door to the plush room that reeked of elegance and pleasure. She breathed a sigh of relief. Jason was not only her boss and friend, he was like the big brother she had never had. In his own subtle way he was taking care of her just like he had been doing since she met him at the Legal Alliance Workshop ten years ago. Jason had been married for 25 years to the love of his life and had two children he adored. His wife, Peggy, was a local attorney who had learned how to have a good work-life balance. She worked at the office three days a week and was home for four days a week. She left work every day by 5 PM, no exceptions. I, once, asked her how she was able to achieve such a feat. Her answer was simple. She said, "I just learned how to say the magic word 'no'. No, I won't be able to work on that today." She was an exceptional attorney and her boss had sensed that her response would not tolerate debate. As a great and irreplaceable asset to the legal firm, they could not risk losing her.

Pharisee unpacked her over-priced custom black LV luggage because she hated living out of a suitcase even for one day. She could never find anything that way. Most of the things packed were travel clothes, items that would not require ironing. She brought pieces that could double for day and night. First, on today's agenda was to shower and take a walk down to the local deli. It was one that she often frequented when she was in town. Washington DC had a monopoly on good restaurants, good music, and interesting things to do. Her plans included spending at least two days at the Smithsonian museum. There was no way she could see everything in one visit. Her "to do" list, also, encompassed a visit to the Grand Central Station and to get some shopping done. She would be open to "whatever" on this trip. Pharise stepped out of the hotel. The northern wind was a little brisk. She wrapped her arms around her body to keep the wind from blowing her clothes open. No one else walking seemed to notice the breezy cool weather. But, she was a southern girl and she was use to hot humid days. The wind was a welcomed visitor. The street was filled with people walking with a mission. Today, she was not that person. She was there to enjoy herself and she would not be in a hurry. She was learning that she did not always have to be on fast-forward. Her goal was to slow down on this trip and just enjoy.

The deli was almost filled to capacity, but she still wanted a window seat. The smell of baked bread welcomed her at the door. Enduring a short wait, she was led to a table that allowed her to watch the happenings on the street. She loved people-watching, something she rarely had an opportunity to do. She and her sister, Felice, spent most of Memphis in May, a local festival, just watching people having what they considered to be fun. Most of them were too enamored with the local beers, daiquiris and colodas, and other fruity drinks with sexual names to even know their name or where they were. She ordered her meal, a roast beef sandwich with spicy mustard, a side salad and jalapeños on the side. The deli had the best roast beef. She took one bite, closed her eyes and leaned her head slightly back enjoying the succulent taste until her internal antenna went on full alert. Someone was watching her. She had always had what her mother called a sixth sense. She couldn't quite discern if this was good or bad. Most of the time, it felt just good old creepy. Her gaze took in the occupants of the room. She wasn't from here, so who would know her? There at the bar was a good looking brother. She wasn't in the market for a man or a relationship. A man would just complicate her life, which she did not need or want. He looked familiar from his profile, but she couldn't see his face. Surely, she didn't know him and resumed eating. She was enjoying every bite of her meal. Pharise opened her eyes again to see a waitress standing over the table with a glass of wine. The waitress, who spoke with a nasal dialect, said "the gentlemen at the bar sent this to the table". She hadn't drunk anything with liquor in it for the last fifteen years of her life. Pharise wasn't quite sure if she looked like she needed a drink or if this was a come on. Whatever the reason, she couldn't accept it. "Please let the gentleman know that I don't drink alcoholic beverages. Tell him, "thank you for the gesture." The waitress quickly left. She finished her meal and was just settling the bill when the waitress reappeared. "Ms., the gentleman wanted to give you his business card and asked if you would please give him a call". She was about to get a little unnerved with this guy when she turned the card over. It was the most elegant business card that she had ever seen, but this was DC and people probably did everything in a big way. The black and gold card embossed in gold print simply said Roxel C. Stapleton, CEO and owner of Allegory

Medical. He was the owner of the multi-billion dollar company. This was the very same company that she had investigated and would continue to investigate. Pharise's eyes gleaned the bar, but he had already left. Her intuition had not failed her. It was true. She had seen him before. The last time she had seen him, he was angry, specifically at her. People said that she was blunt with a dash of cynicism, although they probably didn't use those exact words. Pharise had simply asked some hard questions and Roxel had taken it personally, as if she was attacking the integrity of his company. Actually, she was. That's what she did and up until recently Pharise had been pretty good at it. She wasn't sure if Roxel remembered her or if she was someone he was interested in. Whatever the motive behind her receiving his business card, she would make it her business to find out. Pharise slipped the card in her over-sized MK purse. She was an "in your face kind of girl", a straight shooter. She didn't have time to play games. Pharise doubled the tip for the waitress, thanked her for the delicious meal and left.

Roxel sat in his late model Lexus in the parking lot across the street from the deli. He should have left 30 minutes ago if he wanted to be on time for his meeting. He had just dialed the number to his office to inform them that he would be late when she walked out of the deli. He was startled back to reality when the voice on the other end of the telephone called his name again for the umpteenth time. "Yes, this is me. Let the staff and the visitors know that I have been unavoidably detained and I won't be able to make the meeting. Yes, I realize that I am the one that called the meeting, but something has come up and I'm across town. Please reschedule and send the visitors a nice gift to reiterate my apologies. Thanks, I owe you big time Sam." Sam was short for Samantha. Samantha was his administrative assistant and someone he could not live without. She held his fragile life together with a phone and a laptop. At this very moment, he felt like a stalker. He watched Pharise to see what hotel she was staying in. It had been about a year and a half since he had seen her stroll into his plant causing his employees to question their safety. There was something about Pharise Mallard that held him captive and at the same time kept him off balance. Frankly, he didn't like her. She had all but accused him of having a deplorable and an unsafe work environment. It was obvious that she was on some type of ego trip. And, what really pissed him off was that she had failed to do her homework. He had to admit that his company had issues with equipment and processes, but he had never intentionally placed anyone at risk. In fact, he modeled his company's safety policy after national standards and had often gone beyond this to guarantee their safety. He was going to find out what was driving Pharise Mallard and why she was targeting his plant.

A light drizzle had begun. She walked so quickly back to the hotel that it might have appeared as if she was running. The mid day sun was now hidden by low hanging clouds. The change in the weather also signaled a change in her mood. Pharise would delay her outdoor activities today and relax with one of her favorite romance novels. She silently prayed that her dark mood would pass and at least give her a reprieve for the afternoon Pharise came to DC to enjoy herself and she would, even if it killed her. As she entered the hotel's revolving door, she turned around to look. Again, she had the sinking feeling that she was being watched. She wondered, "Am I being paranoid on top of being depressed?" She discarded the familiar feeling as she stepped onto the elevator. Just a few more floors and she would be back in her room as her back massaged the back of the elevator. She wondered what direction her life would be taking, sensing that there were some big changes on the horizon for her.

Roxel had already missed one meeting. If he didn't hurry back, he would miss a second one. This was so not like him. He watched her sprint down the street trying to escape the light rain. He had come to grips with his feelings for this woman. He was angry with her to say the least. He didn't know anything about her, but he wanted her gone from DC. She signified trouble with a capital "T". When she spoke people listened. She made what she said seem biblical. He could tell that she was an expert at her job. However, her analysis of his plant proved that she was having an off week or possibly an off year. She believed the allegations and made assumptions that were incorrect. To add fuel to the fire, she had sought out the most disgruntled and least experienced employees to interview. The information she had extracted from them was useless and irrelevant. That hadn't stopped her from preparing a safety risk analysis that indicated that Allegory was not only unsafe, but negligent. There had been no supporting evidence on which she based this unfounded analysis. Yes, he would make it his business to get her to leave on the first plane flying out of DC just in case she was there to stir up more trouble for his company.

Chapter 2

PHARISE WAS SUMMONED from reading the best romance novel she
had read in years by the ringing telephone. The novel had suspense,
mystery and romance all wrapped up in one. The romance scenes were way
past erotic. Her love life was in a serious drought and had been for years.
She wasn't complaining, just stating a fact. She wondered who this could
be calling her; for goodness sake she was on vacation.

"Hello" she stated. There was a muffled voice on the other end of the
telephone, "Ms. Mallard, this is an employee at Allegory. I was unaware
that you were back in DC. Will you be returning to our plant on this visit
or are you here on some other business? The hairs on her neck suddenly
stood up. She wondered who this was calling her to get all in her business.
She slowly exhaled before speaking. "Sir, how did you find out that I was
in DC and why would you believe that I would visit Allegory? She thought
he had hung up when she didn't hear anything. There was no sound.
Then, he spoke. "My information comes to me from a variety of sources,
Ms. Mallard. I was hoping that we would not see you for a while. Your
coming affects our livelihood. We consider you a threat to our wealth and
one that we will not tolerate. Do you know how long we have worked to
get things the way we need them so that we can make a lucrative living?
No, you wouldn't know. As long as you are here in DC, that pretty boy
CEO is going to wish he never would have acquired Allegory Medical. It
is our intent to make his life a living hell." There was more silence. "Ms.
Mallard, you know you are just a pawn in our little game. We used you
and your little safety analysis to gain a sympathetic ear from the corporate
office and the Board of Directors. He let out a sarcastic laugh. If you get in
our way, then you will simply become expenditure. I hope we understand
each other". The next thing she heard was a dial tone.

She held the telephone for a few minutes, she wasn't sure how long. She finally spoke out loud, "I can't believe that I have been threatened by someone from Allegory Medical." She didn't take threats well. Not only that, her safety analysis, which she thought had been right on target had been biased. It revealed the results that this group had intended for those reading the report to see. In other words, she had been made a fool of by some sabotaging group at the plant. She suddenly didn't feel so well. Pharise didn't like the arrogant man who was both CEO and interim Plant Manager. He appeared to be hard and uncompromising and he was a hot head. From what she could tell from the previous visits to the facility, it seemed that the employee's loyalty was based both on fear and respect. She had two calls to make and she didn't think that she would enjoy either.

Chapter 3

PHARISE TELEPHONED JASON on his private number at the office and his cell phone, but didn't get an answer at either. She left a voice mail on both. She tried his home number, which she rarely called out of respect to Peggy. She hated to disturb him once he got home. However, this call was urgent. Pharise needed to get this information to Jason. It wasn't that she truly feared that something bad would happen to her, she really couldn't answer that. The man who made the threat on the telephone had enunciated each word so that she would be clear that he was in no way making an idle threat. Peggy picked up the telephone on the third ring. The words emptied out of Pharise's mouth so fast that they begin running together. Peggy said, "Hold on Pharise, what is going on?" "I'm sorry, it's work related. Is Jason there because I really need to talk with him"? You sound a little shaken up, she said. "Yea, well, that's because I am. Some wacko just threatened me". Peggy told her to hold on while she went to get Jason and he picked up immediately. "What's going on Pharise? Who threatened you and how is it related to work?

Pharise repeated what the anonymous caller had said. Jason then spoke slowly, which more than not grated on her nerves. "So, someone or some group influenced the unfavorable report you completed on Allegory Medical. It was more than interesting that it was the union who had handpicked the employees. They guaranteed that they were model workers and who would tell it like it was. But she wondered what purpose they would have in sabotaging things around the plant. It simply made no sense that they would cause injuries to their co-workers.

Jason sighed, "I am going to call a private investigator who is also a friend. After that, I am going to contact the Department of Labor and file a complaint against some of the employees." Jessie Rice, career lawman, was as thorough as they came. He worked for the FBI until he retired and then opened his own private investigation business. Jason said that he was certain that Jessie would be able to provide Pharise with a body guard while she was there.

"I'm on vacation and there won't be anyone following me around and getting in my way. He won't be able to infiltrate the plant unless we have the cooperation of the CEO who is also temporarily acting as the plant manager." Pharise knew that it would not be easy to get his permission. Roxel had given Pharise the distinct feeling that he did not particularly like any of them from Durem Consultants.

"Yea, well I got the same feeling", said Jason. "Well, he is just going to have to get over it, if he doesn't want to receive any more safety citations or be closed down. I don't expect him to be filled with joy on our suggestion of this course of action, but I do believe that he will cooperate. From the little I know about him, the success of his company is paramount". Jason sounded really sure about this. Jason was always a believer. She wasn't so sure if she was one.

Pharise said, "I have his business card and I'll call when I hang up from you". She conveniently left out the part that she had kind of seen Roxel earlier at the deli. Pharise couldn't quite remember where she put the card. "Where is that blasted thing?" She didn't know if she needed ginkoba or a B12 injection. Her memory wasn't worth a flip, she thought as she searched her purse for the third time, finally finding it at the bottom. After dialing his number, the fifth ring escalated the call to his voice mail. Her first inclination was to hang up and not leave a message. That wasn't an option. Some maniac had threatened her. The voice on the phone belonged to someone who had a personal vendetta against her and wasn't beyond doing bodily harm. She planned to derail it. "Hello, Roxel. This is Pharise Mallard and it is imperative that you contact me. I have recently received some additional information surrounding events occurring at your plant and the safety analysis done by our company." There, she had done it. She left a number in which she could be reached. Pharise would have to wait until he retrieved his messages and called back. His extreme dislike for her might become an obstacle in Pharise getting that call, since he had sent his business card over to her earlier, that gave her some hope.

Sleep had been her enemy for the past few weeks. In fact, she almost dreaded the night. It signaled the recurrent nightmares she had been having of someone chasing her. In the last few dreams, she had been chased by an older man and woman. She scurried through the city driving like a bat out of hell trying to get away. The couple driving the older gray sedan seemed to be going at a much slower pace, but they never lost sight of her and she never lost sight of them. In the dream, she looked in the rear view mirror and her image reflected back at her. It was a person who appeared frantic and haggard. The elderly couple had blank looks on their faces. They never seemed to get close to her, but she was unable to ditch them no matter how fast she drove. The place that she was driving was unfamiliar. However, it seemed that somehow she knew where she was going. Lately, when she woke up from her dreams she always felt tired with a sense of dread that surrounded her like a death shroud. On occasion, she had woken having a full blown panic attack. Since she lived alone, she had learned to manage them by slowing her breathing until her heart ceased racing.

She was not quite sure how long she had slept when she heard the phone ringing. She hesitated answering the unknown number, but remembered she was expecting a call from Roxel. Pharise picked up the receiver slowly and paused before saying anything. She exhaled, "Yes, who is this?" a voice so smooth and sensual seeped through the phone. Pharise Mallard, this is Roxel and I am returning your call." It was clear that he had delegated their association to some step slightly above enemy because he was using her entire name. "Yes, I called to let you know that we believe that some of the information contained in the safety analysis we submitted may have been distorted while other information may have been blatant lies".

"Really? And, you came to this conclusion, how?" he stated cynically. "You submitted a bunch of lies and you think that everything should be alright?"

Now she was fuming because of this arrogant and egotistical man. She counted to ten to lower her heart rate for the second time today. Pharise then explained that she had received a threatening telephone call earlier that day and that the muffled male voice indicated that the recent safety incidents were not all accidents. Someone was sabotaging things at the plant. Whatever, their motive, real people were getting hurt.

She was stunned that he had not uttered one word? Was the almighty Roxel speechless? She doubted that he was ever at a loss for words. After what seemed like eternity, he asked, "Where are you Ms. Mallard?" Oh, we were back to titles now, she thought. He must be really peeved. "I'm staying at the Renaissance Hotel downtown." "Who knows you are here in Washington and why are you here?" Well, she thought, both of those were really great questions. No one knew she was there except Jason, his wife, and Olivia, Jason's assistant. She rattled off the names and almost forgetting-- you, Roxel, you know that I am in Washington.

Roxel knew that he didn't have a handle on his emotions at this point. "Ms. Mallard, are you suggesting that I am the responsible party of these threats?" If she believed this, then she was crazier than he thought. Pharise chose her words carefully. She needed his help to get to the bottom of things. "No, I don't believe that you are the culprit. However, someone did threaten me. In addition, they alluded that they were not finished and there would be more accidents. Somehow, my being in the plant hampered some of their plans. They stated that they did not intend for that to happen again. My question to you is why would your workers, who appeared pretty loyal, want to disrupt production and cause injuries?" Her questions really got Roxel to thinking. Things were not adding up and he had a feeling that he knew some of the employees who were taking the lead on this. Roxel believed that he was a good interim manager and a fair boss. Furthermore, he considered loyalty was an attribute that there was an over abundance of at the plant. "Ms. Mallard, I really can't answer either of those questions because I just don't know". Pharise could detect the anguish in his voice as well as the disappointment.

She wanted to first clear the air. "Mr. Stapleton, I'm quite aware of your huge dislike for me, but I am not your enemy. I only came here to do a job based on complaints regarding safety at the facility. It seems that I was intentionally given erroneous information that has shed an unfavorable light on your company. And for that, I will apologize. I will contact the Department of Labor on tomorrow to amend the analysis and re-investigate the allegations."

"First, Roxel said, let's move past these last names and going forward I hope that we can be on a first name basis," he stated. "Agreed?"

"That's fine," Pharise mumbled.

"Second, although you may not be my enemy, I can't delegate you as a friend just yet. What room are you staying in?"

"Why would you need to know that?" she said.

He somehow knew that she wouldn't be forthcoming with that information. He would just have to do things his way. "Never mind," he said, while entering the lobby of the Renaissance Hotel. He casually slipped the bell hop a fifty and he was happy to sing out the room number. He hadn't quite figured out why he was so drawn to her. She kept him on edge when they were in each other's presence. He wanted to find out who was sabotaging things and why and the answers would have to begin with Pharise. He knocked on the door while juggling the telephone with the other hand. He couldn't remember where he had left his Bluetooth. It was much easier to multi-task with it.

"Who is it?" Pharise yelled. She wondered who was at her hotel door. She wasn't expecting company and that feeling of dread begin to inch itself over her. Before she started going full speed ahead panicking, Roxel said, "It's me," Roxel.

Chapter 4

PHARISE LOOKED THROUGH the peep hole and confirmed that it was him. "What are you doing here? You just don't show up at a woman's door unannounced and uninvited. Did your mother never tell you that?"

Roxel simply said, "We need to talk and I am too wired to go home. Will you please open the door?" Pharise had changed into a short lounger that revealed more than it hid. She had a fetish for intimate sleepwear. She quickly grabbed the lomanve blue silk robe. She removed the safety latch and opened the door. Roxel stood at the door momentarily at a loss for words. She was more stunning than he remembered. His eyes headed south and lingered. He simply nodded and attempted to speak, but the words came out in a strangled noise.

She wondered what was wrong with him, until she glanced down following his gaze. She had failed to tie the robe adequately and her revealing nightie was the focus of his attention. While tying the sash on her robe she said, "Why are you here and how did you manage to find out what room I was in?" She knew that resourceful people could gain access to all kinds of things. That's what she was afraid of.

Once he pulled his tongue back into the recesses of his mouth and lifted his head, he simply said "I was in the neighborhood. And like you said, we needed to talk about the threats that were made. We, also, need to figure out how you fit into this puzzle. You need to retract that safety analysis first thing tomorrow morning. Then, I can contact someone to do an internal investigation into the recent string of accidents. I can let you know the results of all the findings. Is there an address or e-mail address that I can forward you this information?"

Roxel hadn't given her as much as an iota of space to interject one single word. Pharise remained calm as he thoroughly gave his opinion of how things would proceed. He hadn't anticipated that she would want to find out why she had been used to further someone's agenda. He hadn't considered that she was the one being threatened and that she might want to find out by whom. "Roxel Stapleton, you underestimate my investigative abilities. In addition, you have misjudged me by thinking that I will tuck my tail and run because I won't. I realize that my presence might create a slightly tense working environment. So, I assure you that I will stay out of your way as much as possible. However, I am not leaving until we have uncovered who is responsible for the recent accidents and who threatened me. I hope that we understand each other." A slight smile turned the corners of her mouth.

He wished he could wipe the smirk right off her face. Did she really believe that they would be able to work together without killing each other? One thing he was certainly aware of and that was he had an unfathomable sexual attraction to her. He couldn't quite understand it and was certain that she didn't even have a clue. Both of them were standing within a foot of each other in her hotel room, which suddenly had gotten smaller and warmer, holding each other's gaze. They were like two year olds. They tried to see who could stare the other one down the longest. It was late and he was hungry. He would allow her to have this little victory. He ceased the stare-down and turned his head, taking in the stylishness of the room. "This is a very nice room. Is it for business or pleasure?" The words came out all wrong, he thought.

"Both", she said, without even a hint of elaboration. The tension in the room was thick enough to cut with a knife. This arrogant controlling man was too easy on the eyes. He was definitely sexy all dressed up. His nose flared when he got worked up. Those hazel eyes outlined in a grayish tint seemed to be able to look straight through her. His coloring reminded her of the New Orleans's creoles. It was a grayish dark coloring with hints of gold highlights in his skin. Yea, this playboy was good looking to say the least and she was going to hate working with him as much as he would hate working with her. "Roxel, we're going to have to move past our dislike for each other. And because I have caused you a great deal of grief, I sincerely want to help." She shook her head at the absurdity of this entire situation.

He looked deeply into her big doe-like brown eyes that slanted upwards slightly and what he saw revealed that she was not only sincere, but deeply sorry. "I accept your apology," Roxel said in a husky voice never taking his eyes off of her face that was without make-up. In fact she was a little disheveled and looked as if she had been asleep. "Did I wake you up?" he asked as if the question puzzled him as to why she would be sleeping at seven o'clock in the evening while his eyes took in everything in the luxury suite.

"Yea, I was. The rain had me in a funk which I couldn't shake. I dozed off while reading." She dared not tell him what she was reading. She didn't want him to think that she was desperate for a man because she was not. At this point in her life, she chose to be alone. She had too many issues and baggage to take into a relationship.

"Since you are all apologetic and all, Ms. Mallard, I have a favor to ask of you."

She had to tilt her head backwards to look into the eyes of this man, who appeared to be about six feet and some. "I'm all ears, what is it?"

"I am starving, do you mind if I order room service and we sit down and strategize what will be our course of action?"

She wasn't getting any bad vibes from him and didn't believe that he was a lunatic or serial killer. "Order away, Roxel." I need to change into something more appropriate after she looked down at her attire again. After returning to her bedroom, she changed into a blue silk camisole set. To a casual observer, it might seem a little risqué. It had been given to her by her best friend, Angel, a couple of years back. She was half dressed to say the least and had carried on a conversation with him, already, for more than thirty minutes.

"Why change, your outfit isn't bothering me. In fact, I think it is quite appealing. I promise you that I will not complain about what you're wearing. Remember, I'm the one who interrupted your *sleep* and you should be able to wear anything you like in your own hotel room". *He smiled inwardly.*

She wondered if he was kidding. She simply rolled her eyes at him, grabbed something from a drawer and headed for the bathroom.

He murmured, "No use of crying over spilled milk" as he picked up the receiver and ordered from his favorite Thai restaurant. He was grateful that they delivered. His order included enough food for 4 people. He was famished. He ordered sweet and sour soup, spring rolls, crab wontons, an order of basil fried rice with shrimp and one with chicken and an apple crumb cake and cheese cake with blueberry topping.

He removed his suit jacket and hung it over the champagne colored chaise which was long enough for him to stretch out. He didn't watch much TV because he rarely had the time. He was in the process of answering the twenty four new e-mails on his cell phone when Pharise emerged from the bathroom. She was drop dead gorgeous. She had unwrapped her curly hair that hung down past her shoulders. She was wearing linen shorts that came mid-way her thigh and a linen tank top that were both some sort of hybrid between mint green and pale blue.

"I see you made yourself comfortable. What did you order to eat?"

He rattled off what he'd ordered as she simply took in how comfortable he had gotten. His tie was loosened, his jacket draped the chaise and he had on what appeared to be reading glasses.

While in the bathroom, she'd taken a quick shower, brushed her teeth, and freshened up hoping this would resurrect her from this crazy mood she was still in. Roxel's mere presence had helped some. However, when one of these moods came, it was hard to get over it. She answered the door looking like a reject from a porn movie. She prayed that she and Roxel would learn to at least tolerate each other. Pharise knew that, although it had been a while since she had talked to God, He still heard her prayers. She would earnestly pray tonight.

Chapter 5

PHARISE, IF SHE was honest with herself, knew that she was emotionally fragile with her moods vacillating between highs and lows. These mood swings impacted her relationships, with family and friends and she didn't know how to get past them. Pharise stared at Roxel who was busy texting on the phone. He hadn't even noticed she was back in the room. Although she couldn't quite figure out the weird vibes in the room, she knew something was going on between the two of them besides their blatant dislike and mistrust of each other. Life appeared to have thrown a curve ball to both of them. They would have to tolerate each other and it would start with them being able to tolerate sharing a meal, discussing things through, and being in close proximity of one another for a little while longer. Pharise, although she considered herself to be able to socialize with the best of them, was a loner by nature. People gravitated towards her, but not the other way around. Lately, she had been shutting her loved ones out. This vacation, she hoped, would help her get things into perspective and prioritize her life. Things didn't appear to look real good right now, but she would keep the hope that a change was in the air.

"How long do you plan to stand there and daydream about whatever has that haunting look on your face?" He'd known the moment she re-entered the room. The hair on the back of his neck stood up and her fragrance preceded her. "You were really deep in thought and I hated to interrupt what's going on in that pretty little head of yours, but the food is getting icicles on it. I don't want to beat a dead horse, but I'm starving. In just a few minutes you will have to utilize those CPR classes when I faint from hunger."

That gorgeous smile showed up again. She hadn't noticed the unilateral deep dimple in his left cheek and the deep recesses of the cleft in his chin.

il

His teeth were perfectly white with the most sensual lips she had seen in a long time. It seemed that he was in the mood for some good natured teasing. Pharise would indulge him tonight and let him get away with it. "Oh, well then, I need to definitely apologize for delaying our meal and I left my CPR card back in Memphis along with all my other nursing credentials. So, if you plan on fainting dead away, I might not be your girl." She laughed at the thought of him fainting. That really would be something.

The food was absolutely delicious. She couldn't recall eating this much in a long time. The spicier the food, the more she liked it and this food was spicy taken to another level. The spring rolls were the best ever. The shell was so light and flaky. She was picking up the crumbs with her fingers. The plum sauce was not the typical heavy syrupy kind. The consistency was a lot thinner and the flavors were not overwhelming. Roxel had found the way to her heart. She was definitely impressed by his ability to choose food that she really enjoyed. And he definitely was starving. He put down two generous plates of food easily. She leaned back in her chair. It felt as if she needed to unbutton the first button of her fitted shorts, but she would wait until her uninvited dinner companion left.

"How was everything?" he asked. His eyes twinkled with mischief. He was daring her to lie and say that she hadn't enjoyed the meal, but she couldn't deflate his huge ego. "It was hands down the best meal that I have had in the last few years. It, almost, makes up for the fact that you barged into my hotel room", she said with a light chuckle.

"Again, I apologize for that, but I'm not sorry I came." Roxel looked at her with a heated gaze before he changed the subject and the fire in his eyes disappeared. "Let's discuss our next move and figure out how we will deal with those culprits in this dangerous game." He hadn't really considered why he had ended up at her hotel, paid for her room information, and was still in her room two hours later. He felt so comfortable being here. Roxel had gotten more work done in her hotel room than he had the entire day at the office. The chaise was extremely comfortable. He was a big man and it wasn't often that he found a chair that didn't cause him to feel the stress that was always evident in his shoulders. He had loosened the tie that seemed to have tightened like a noose as his stress level for the day had increased. Pharise had such an easy going spirit, although he guessed she was in some type of personal turmoil. Roxel didn't have time to play mind games or try to figure out what made her tick. He would accept her help and the resources from her company to find the perpetrators. She could then return back to the south and continue her life as it had been before. However, Roxel had to admit that she was growing on him in such a short period of time. She had a wicked sense of humor that had him constantly smiling.

His mind wandered to pleasant thoughts of his mother. His mother would think that he had been hit in the head or something if she could see him now. That reminded him; he needed to call his mother to check on her. He hadn't spoken with her in two days. He was definitely a momma's boy, even though he loved and respected his dad. His mother was his friend and confident. He had made great choices for their dinner and Pharise had enjoyed it immensely. He was waiting on her to deny it, but she hadn't. That was a good sign. She wasn't a liar.

Chapter 6

ROXEL CALLED ROOM SERVICE and had the food cleared. He didn't want her to awaken to the odors from old food. They moved from the dining area to the sitting area. The room was definitely suited for business and pleasure. Pharise had given him the information to the private investigator that Jason had recommended. They had attempted to contact Jessie Rice by phone, but had to resort to leaving a message on his voice mail. First thing tomorrow, she would contact her source at the Department of Labor to amend the safety analysis. Roxel planned to have security beefed up in every area inside the plant, including the perimeter. Their security company should be able to handle that. He would also speak to the union stewards to find out what were the major concerns at the plant. This should give him an idea of what and who was really behind the accidents. Roxel would, also, set up a town hall meeting to listen to the most vocal employees. He was certain that at least one of them would slip up, out of anger or frustration, and give them some valuable information. "How are you going to stay out of the line of fire? It's obvious that you may be a target. I would like to suggest that you get a body guard", Roxel offered. Pharise emphatically said, "That won't work for me." She would not become a victim. Her vacation would continue as planned and Pharise would not allow the perpetrators to bully her into hiding out or having to be shadowed. She had to catch herself from yelling out these thoughts. It was obvious she had a short fuse when pushed into a corner. He would just have to figure out another way to protect her from those who threatened her. It was likely that she would be totally pissed off if she found out, but that was just too bad. So, Roxel would need to make sure that she didn't. She was too ornery for her own good. That was just one of the things that he liked about her. Under different circumstances, he probably would ask her out on a date, but he didn't mix business with pleasure and it would be useless since she lived hundreds of miles away. However, he was definitely interested in Pharise Mallard if he had to say so himself. She was what the plant workers called "hot tamale". She had a fiery temper and a hot body. That was a heck of a combination.

Pharise interrupted Roxel's zoning out by saying, "Roxel, it's getting late and we need to get an early start tomorrow."

Roxel was stunned. "Are you kicking me out of your hotel room, he said?" he was looking at her like she had a horn planted in the middle of her head.

Pharise was no push over. She simply said, "Yes, I am. If you don't leave now, I am going to fall asleep on you anyway. I'm exhausted. I need at least eight hours of sleep every night. If I don't get it, then I am a force to be reckoned with," she said as she gently pushed him toward the door.

He picked up his jacket and grabbed his brief case. He had never been put out of a woman's hotel room before in his life. This was definitely a first for him.

She laughed when she registered the shock on his face. "What? I guess the pretty boy has never been put out of a woman's room before now." Pharise was still smiling at his bewildered look. He simply stopped walking and she almost plowed into his back. His six-four and two hundred plus muscled frame would be like hitting a brick wall. He quickly maneuvered her soft pliant body to keep her from falling. His hands rested below her waist and not quite at her hips. He made her nervous being so up close and personal. Well, good. She made him nervous too and it served her right for putting him out. He simply stood there refusing to move his large hands. She looked into his eyes and she could see what he didn't say. There was a spark, simmering, waiting to be gently fanned.

He simply said, "thank you for allowing me to interrupt your evening. I haven't been this much at ease in a long time. You were great company. Have a good night", he said in the huskiest voice she had ever heard.

Shivers ran down her spine and Roxel hadn't even done anything that one might consider sensual or had he? He opened the door, turned around for the last time and gave her a wink and told her to lock up. She gently closed the door and leaned against it, finally able to get a good breath out. She was startled when he said from the other side of the door, "I'm waiting on you to lock-up". She latched the door and turned the lock. She heard him say, "good night" again and heard his footfalls as he walked down the hall. She heard the elevator chime, the door opened and closed. She walked back into the interior of the brightly colored room and dressed for bed. His scent permeated through the room. It was some kind of mixture of leather, cigars, and musk. It smelled delicious. Hopefully, she would not wrestle with her demons in her sleep tonight. She prayed that she would not have to. It was 12:45 AM when she last peered at the clock on the bedside table. Roxel had been in her room more than four hours. She had definitely enjoyed his company. This was her last thought before she succumbed to a restful sleep.

Chapter 7

$\mathcal{P}$HARISE ARRIVED AT the facility bright and early. Normally, she was not an early riser. Last night, she didn't have a nightmare and she was grateful for that. The alarm clock had gone off at 5 AM. She had forgone hitting the snooze button. She showered and dressed in record time. She changed clothes three times before she found the right outfit to wear. The navy power suit trimmed in pink made her appear slimmer than her size twelve frame. Sleek navy pumps topped off her ensemble. No matter how gray her mood, dressing up always made her feel better. She was out of the hotel at 5:45 AM. It took exactly twenty minutes to drive to Allegory from the hotel. She checked in at a security station that had seen better days, which was located at one of the side entrances to the plant. A driver's license was required to get past security. Roxel was her contact and the guard had called someone in administration to okay her entry while she waited patiently. The arm of the security gate lifted and she rounded the corner and parked in the lot designated for visitors and staff. As she exited her car, she looked around and marveled at the architectural structure that housed Allegory Medical. It was a glass-like structure with dark tinted gold windows. It showcased an intricate and detailed architectural masterpiece with smooth lines and obtuse angles. It seemed somewhat out of place in the semi-industrial area. Cherry blossom trees standing in pairs lined the path that led toward the entrance. The emblem "A" was engraved in the two concrete pillars that flanked the edges of the walkway. Although the facility was not far from the "downtown" area, it was far enough to be beyond walking distance to any of the fancy restaurants, museums, and places were the locals gathered. Each visitor was given a temporary proxy card that allowed them entry. The petite Asian receptionist at the door ushered her to a meeting room, relaying that Mr. Stapleton had left instructions for her to attend the staff briefing that started 5 minutes ago. If she hadn't been detained at security, she would have been on time for the meeting. Pharise slipped in the room quietly. There was now only standing room and she had to stand along the wall with about fifteen other employees. It seemed her entrance had caught the interim plant manager a little off guard because she noticed a slight hesitance in his speech. Certain that no one else had been aware of the pause, she leaned back on the cool wall. Their eyes met briefly and he nodded his awareness of her presence so slightly that no one else would have noticed. He was startling and masculine in his two thousand dollar navy designer athletic cut tailored suit.

He went on to say, "It has come to my attention that we have had a rash of accidents in the last 3 months, which equates to an almost thirty three percent increase, since this time last year. These accidents are not our normal slip, trips, and falls that we usually see. In fact, the accidents that we have recorded have been what can be coined as "freak accidents". Often, there were no witnesses present. It is paramount that we get a handle on what has been going on. We need to become more observant of our employees and address problem equipment quickly. In one incident, a pallet fell from the Mezzanine and injured a worker walking below. My question is why would a pallet be there in the first place? In another instance, a fork lift was left running and rolled into an employee coming out of an office door. It pinned the employee, crushing her leg. In another instance, a guard was broken off one of the conveyors that connected two lines of prosthetic material. The broken guard caused an employee to partially lose a finger and damaged more than $200,000 worth of products. Many of these recent incidents are suspect. I am the first one to admit that we have not done a good enough job keeping our employees safe. Managers and staff, I am holding you partially responsible because we have not kept our eyes and ears open. It is obvious that complacency has been the order of the day for some time. Things are definitely going to have to change if we are to continue to be productive and meet the deadlines for our products. Otherwise, our competition will gain momentum on us. When we fail to get our orders out, not only do we lose money, but we lose the trust of our customers."

As he looked around the room holding the gaze of each person present he said, "That will not happen". Some employees murmured among themselves while others held their heads down. Pharise was simply entranced at the magnitude of his speaking ability and the power he exuded. She jotted down a few notes of things that she had not previously known. Roxel opened the floor for questions. There were a few from staff that seemed genuinely concerned about the recent accidents. Others seemed disinterested, looking as if they wanted to be anywhere else other than this meeting. It was obvious that many of the employees were really loyal, but Pharise got a sinking feeling that some were not and was not impressed by his assessment of events. While her head was still down and she was busy writing, she didn't hear or notice that they had been dismissed and people were leaving the meeting room.

Roxel noticed her immediately when she entered the room, disturbing his train of thought. She was classy in the power suit that mirrored the ones showcased in high-end boutiques. It fit her curvy figure. Navy had never been a favorite color of his on a woman, but to say that she looked good was an understatement. Most of the women Roxel dated were all a certain type, the thin non-descript model type. He had never gone out with a woman that could be described as "stacked." But, Pharise looked absolutely mouth-watering. Her skin was a very light toffee color with hints of gold and orange highlights. Her coloring reminded him of some of his Creole friends that had attended college with him. She was a self-assured woman who wore her independence on her sleeve. That caused them to clash on most occasions. Roxel planned to work on that.

Pharise left the meeting room following the crowd toward the administration area which held the offices of the managers and the support staff. Roxel was engrossed in a conversation with several employees in the hall. She passed him and headed towards John Braxton's office, their labor attorney. John was the one friend Pharise had made during her last visit. She truly liked his fresh assessment of events. John was a brilliant labor attorney. Pharise knocked gently on the outside glass wall. His door was open. He looked up at the same time that she said, "Hey". John got up from behind his desk hurriedly and enveloped his friend in a giant bear hug. Pharise normally wasn't attracted to the European type, but John was good looking in a "big" way. He had the bluest eyes and his hair was peppered with gray. The tiny crow's feet around his eyes appeared when he smiled only added to his masculine appeal. Pharise was no matchmaker, but she couldn't quite figure out why John was single. John confessed that he had been divorced for the last seven years and had been too busy with work to develop any kind of meaningful relationship. Pharise didn't buy this one bit. Relationships were hard. And, if they failed, then it left strong viable individuals often in ruins. He mentioned that his wife had simply said, after he came home after ten one night, that she couldn't do it anymore. His wife no longer wanted to be a corporate widow. She would rather be with someone who made $30,000 a year, knew she was alive, and who made her first in his life. John said he had seen it coming. But for the life of him, he didn't know how to stop it from happening. John knew that everything she said wasn't completely true because she was still unmarried and he paid her a hefty six-figure yearly alimony check. John believed he hadn't chosen his job over his wife. But in retrospect, he knew that by not actively choosing to make her first, he had lost the true love of his life. They hadn't had any children, so that minimized the casualties of their doomed marriage.

Pharise asked, "How's my friend?"

John said that he was fine, although his eyes betrayed him. "It is so good to see you. It's been a while. I didn't know you were coming," he said. They had been keeping in touch by e-mail and face book. On occasions, the two would pick up the telephone and call each other. John knew that she had been having a hard time since her mom's death. Maybe, that was the thing that connected them to each other. It was like they were kindred spirits, both sharing in their own personal pain. They were laughing and enjoying catching up and apparently caught up in the moment when they were interrupted by that husky male voice that had recently began to violate her thoughts. However, she detected a chill in the voice that had been warm on last night. "I didn't know you two were such good friends?" he said. Neither John nor she responded right away. Maybe they weren't real sure whether it was a question or statement. John took the high road and said, "We kind of connected during her last visit when she performed the safety analysis." John told him that he had family back in Memphis that Pharise knew. His smile was huge as he used his hands to give emphasis to what he said. John possessed that same confident posture that Roxel personified. She had seen the two men interact previously and they seemed to have a good relationship. Tension had somehow seeped into the room. Roxel said through tightened lips, "it seems that some people are really good at making lasting impressions." Pharise could see his left eye jump and his chin appeared rigid. "Pharise, may I please see you in my office?" he didn't give her time to respond. He turned on his heels and left the room as arrogantly as he had entered.

Pharise felt like she had been reprimanded by her father for not having ironed his handkerchiefs on Sunday morning. Well, she did what any reprimanded kid would do. She rebelled. Pharise didn't move an inch. In fact, she took a seat and continued her conversation with John. They made plans to catch up more at dinner the next evening. After engaging in a pleasant catch-up with John, Pharise left John's office and headed for the ladies room. Roxel had gotten on her nerves already with his craziness. And, she thought she had mood swings.

Pharise looked in the mirror after straightening her clothes. She failed to recognize the person that looked back at her. Had she changed that much in the last two years? There were dark patches under her eyes that hadn't been there before. Lately, her purchases of concealer to lighten the spots would have earned her stock in the company. About a month after her mom's death she opted for a shoulder length style from the longer curly style she used to wear, mostly because her hair seemed to be coming out from the stress anyway. Her weight had fluctuated at a plus or minus ten pounds since then. But, those were the easy things to spot. However, what a watchful eye couldn't detect was that she was hollow inside. Pharise's therapist had warned her that if she didn't learn to let go of her emotions and deal with the grief, then she wouldn't be able to move forward with her life. She would shed tears, especially in session, but they were few. Her therapist said that it was controlled grieving. She never relinquished control. Others might say that she was a control freak. The jury was still out on this. Maybe, the passing of time was what was needed, since it was the healer of wounds. Either way, she was not in the mood to deal with a self-absorbed jerk.

Roxel left John's office fuming at his display of emotions. That was so totally unlike him. He was in a pretty decent mood until he observed her kissing John on his cheek. It was obvious that they were close. He wondered when this all happened. After searching for Pharise for about ten minutes, he stumbled on her and John. Roxel had been worried that she might have felt alienated, not having anyone there she knew. His plans were to give her an office so that she could have a meeting place to continue her investigation and interview additional employees. His first choice was to place her at the opposite end of the hall, close to the fax and copier and away from most of the staff. She would also be closer to John in that office. However, he felt he needed to rethink this. And while he was at it, he needed to rethink why he acted like a jerk a few minutes earlier.

Pharise made her way to Roxel's office 15 minutes after he had all but ordered her there. His office was huge with a large cherry wood desk that sat directly in front of a large picture window. The room was elegantly decorated with a few personal items and belongings visible. On top of a secretary table in the corner of the room was a picture of a happy family. There was a good looking older couple and two younger couples flanking Roxel, who stood beside what appeared to be his parents. Their smiles were not plastic. They loved each other. That much was evident. That's what was missing from her life, that older loving couple. Her brother and sister were still alive. She adored them both. They were married with families of their own. Her parents passing, especially her mother's death had left a big hole in her heart. She was lost in her own musings when she was startled by his voice. "I am glad you could make it", Roxel said as he exited a hidden bathroom in his office. His face was expressionless and unreadable. She stood there waiting. On what, she didn't know.

"Hey, look I'm sorry for acting like a jerk. I'm usually a lot more charming".

He searched Pharise's face to determine her reaction to what he'd just said.

She didn't know what to say to that, probably because she didn't know enough about him. Maybe, he was having a bad day, she thought. She was about to let him off the hook, when they heard screaming and yelling. She could hear supervisors on the radio asking what was going on. In the hall, she saw everyone running to the plant floor. Roxel took off and Pharise took off right behind him staying close on his heels. They all ran in unison toward a crowd of employees who looked distraught. Some of the ladies had tears in their eyes. There sprawled on the floor was an employee whose leg was awkwardly bent behind her back and at a ninety degree angle. Clearly, she was in excruciating pain as tears flowed silently down her face. Her agonizing moans left all of them in a state of helplessness.

Pharise heard someone calling 911while instructions were given not to move her. Pharise assisted with elevating her head after she started heaving, in case she vomited and held her hand. Her moans of pain tore at them all. Someone handed Pharise a red emergency bag. It looked like a clean break with no sign of external bleeding. She had a few scrapes on her face and arm from the fall. Some of the managers were examining the scissor lift that was almost broken in half from the fall. She asked them to take pictures of the lift. They had begun to rope off the area moving the employees back. It was obvious that this event had stopped production. Employees from other areas were still heading toward the scene while others were milling around. The emergency unit arrived quickly and they rolled her onto a transfer board before sliding her onto the stretcher. A group of them followed them to the waiting ambulance.

Roxel said, "I'm going to follow them in my car and call back to let everyone know how she is doing." Pharise simply nodded her head acknowledging his concern for the employee. She, along with the others, headed back inside after the ambulance sped out of sight with the siren wailing. This accident had all the markings of a deliberate act of sabotage in her book. Scissor lifts didn't usually plummet to the ground and crumble like a can of sardines. Something was amiss and she intended to find out what and who it was.

She went back to the area of the incident with her digital camera. Although she had instructed a safety manager to take pictures, she wanted to make sure it was done. She photographed the scissor lift. Pharise had investigated enough safety accidents that she could tell when something was not accidental. There was a clean cut along the internal legs of the lift as if they had been cut. It was obvious that whoever cut it had made sure that the cut did not go all the way through, so as not to alert the users of the equipment that something was wrong with it. As she looked around the immediate area, she noticed two large screws, which she photographed. The screws were not worn and likely could have not worked themselves out. After examining the lift, it was clear that there were empty screw holes where screws should have been. She had contacted the private investigator, Jessie Rice again while waiting on the ambulance to come. He had been checked in at the security console. She met him in the lobby and briefed him on her suspicions. No one other than Roxel knew why she was at the plant. She escorted Jessie to what now appeared to be a crime scene. Jessie had been able to get in touch with some federal agents who tagged along. She left them and was heading back to Roxel's office to write everything down while it was still fresh. She, also, wanted to download the pictures. An eerie feeling descended over her like someone was watching her. She needed to be careful. These accidents weren't coincidental. She turned searching her surroundings for a clue as to who it was when Pharise saw two employees staring at her with an expression of disdain. She didn't recall who either of them was. They were deep in conversation and turned as two other men approached them. All four men then left and headed for the men's locker room. Their backs were to her. An employee who she interviewed during an earlier visit approached and Pharise inquired about the employees. The employee identified one as Ben Frist, a union steward, and another one as Jake Towns, the union president. She was unable to identify the other two workers. Pharise noted this information and wondered why the union would be involved. She didn't have any answers today, but she was determined to get them.

Pharise was sitting at the desk downloading the images when Rice and his friends came in. It's was obvious that someone tampered with that scissor lift. They sliced the legs so it wouldn't cut through. However, once someone got on it and began moving it would come tumbling down. Their back up plan was unscrewing the screws so that they could work themselves out from the movement. Either way, it was a set up for disaster.

It was late when they left. All of their cars were parked near the front of the facility. This had been a long day. Pharise got in her car and buckled up, her heart was still pumping loudly in her chest. She hoped the employee would be alright. It was obvious she had at least one break in her leg, maybe more. She hadn't heard from Roxel since he left. John had stuck his head in Roxel's door before leaving, but that had been an hour ago. She pulled off slowly, but didn't miss noticing two men sitting in a dark sedan about fifty feet away. She couldn't make out their faces, but knew that they were watching her. She prayed that they would stay put and not start anything. Luckily, Jessie and the other men were still with her and had pulled out behind her. Hopefully, everything would be fine. They wouldn't dare take a chance with those men.

Chapter 8

ROXEL HAD ACTUALLY beaten the ambulance to the local hospital. He paced back and forth like a caged lion. Initially, every few minutes he had gone back to the receptionist desk and inquired as to whether the employee had arrived and the answer was always, "no." The last time the lady at the desk, noticing how agitated he was, told him she would let him know when they arrived. He was forced to make two of the most difficult phone calls in his life. He chose to call the employee's family first. This normally was a job for the safety officer, but he felt obligated to do it. He had spoken with the employee's sister and apprised her of what had happened. She told him she was on her way and would be bringing the employee's two children with her. He had known the employee for six years. She was a valuable and hard working. After reassuring her sister that he would remain there, he made the second call.

Roxel thought his father was a little on the anal side. He had taken over as CEO of the company seven years ago after his dad had a heart attack and decided to retire. His father had gone to a four year program at a local university and obtained a degree in prosthetics and orthotics. At that time, there were only a few people seeking degrees in this new profession. His father had worked for a local small company with no desire to expand their services or clientele. He left the company and used the $20,000 in his 401k to start the business. The first couple of years had been rough. People were still content in wearing the antiquated prosthetics that were not functional. He went to hospitals and physician offices educating them on the new technology and the benefits from obtaining custom orthotics and prosthetics. Slowly, the business began to grow and today it was a multi-billion dollar company with a great history of having excellent products. Inwardly, he believed he had let his father down. Although the company was insured, the rash of accidents would not fare well in the mind of its customers. The previous plant manager had been transferred to their Albuquerque plant and he had stepped in until that could hire a new one.

His dad answered the telephone abruptly, signaling that he might not be in a good mood. "Hey dad, it's me, Roxel. I called to let you know we had another serious accident. This one seems to be more serious than the others. It appears that the employee's leg might be broken in several places and I don't have a clue about what other injuries she might have. It looks like someone tampered with the scissor lift that she was working on when it just collapsed. He went on to tell him what they had observed on the scene. He let him know that he was at the hospital waiting for the employee to arrive. He could tell his father was angry because he was silent. After a few minutes, he asked how the employee was doing. His father loved the plants and the employees. "Dad, I know that you are disappointed in this situation. I assure you that we will get to the bottom of it and find out who is sabotaging the business. I am asking that you have a little faith in me right now. I probably don't deserve it, but I can sure use it." His dad simply said, "Find out who the culprit is and contact the authorities so that formal charges can be brought up against whoever it is. Know this; I don't care who it is, manager, employee, engineer, or scientist. Call me back when you find out more about how the employee is doing." Roxel said, "I will", but his father had already placed the phone back onto the receiver because all he heard was a dial tone sounding in his ear.

The ambulance finally arrived. The employee was taken immediately to be examined, get an MRI and some x-rays according to the nurse. He had been waiting over an hour and a half when her family arrived and sat and waited with him to hear from the doctors. He had gone to the cafeteria to get something to eat for the children and her sister. He grabbed a couple of coffee for himself. He remembered he hadn't eaten anything today. He was starving, but was too worked up to eat. He would grab something on the way home if it wasn't too late.

It was 1:30 in the morning when he walked out of the hospital's emergency department. The employee had to be admitted. According to the doctor, she had multiple fractures in her leg, ankle, and pelvis. She had on a long leg cast on the right side and a brace on her right side to her thigh. According to the doctor who came out to talk with him and her family, she had a long road to recovery. They were hopeful that she should be fine. His dad had suggested opening up a bank account in her name to pay for incidentals. He would have Sam do that first thing tomorrow. It had been a long night. They weren't any closer to finding out the person or persons orchestrating the incidents. Whoever it was had better find a huge rock to hide up under because Roxel was going to hunt him down like a rogue dog.

Roxel had been driving for the last hour with no destination in mind. He had the safety officer to contact those back at the plant to let them all know how the employee was doing. Most of the first shift had left along with the day shift managers. Sam had offered to tell him that Pharise had left late and that some of her guests had arrived and they had gone out in the plant and looked around. He knew it was probably the private investigator they had talked about. Before he knew it, he was at the Renaissance hotel for the second night in a row. He leaned his head on the steering wheel wondering what he was doing there. It was after three o'clock in the morning. Moments later he stepped out of the car convincing himself that he needed to give Pharise an update on the employee and to see if the investigator had found out anything else. "Yea, he said, this was definitely a business visit." Roxel's life, as it had been, was slowly unraveling like a rebellious piece of thread in your favorite garment. It was obvious that there wasn't a thing that he could do about it except hang on in there for the ride.

He softly knocked on the door trying not to disturb the other the guests. Unconsciously, he leaned his head forward on the door obscuring her ability to look out of the peep hole.

It took a few minutes for Pharise to hear the knocking on her door. She had come home, showered and gone straight to bed. "Yes, she said, in a very sexy sleepy voice".

"Pharise, it's me, Roxel. Please open up."

He sounded miserable. She heard weariness and distress in his voice. There was no way she wouldn't open the door. Again, she was disheveled from a fitful rest and she was not even mad that her sleep had been interrupted. She opened the door and she looked into his glazed eyes. In them she saw frustration. He only maintained eye contact for a few seconds before he dropped his head again. He looked utterly defeated.

"Roxel, come on in. You look dead tired. What are you doing here?"

Surely, she wouldn't even understand that he couldn't think of anywhere else to go. Most women would make way too much out of that, but he knew Pharise wouldn't. "I came to tell you about the employee and to hear what happened with the investigator."

She simply stared at him hoping he didn't even believe that lie. It was filled with holes. He could have just as easily waited a few hours to relay that information and to tell her about the employee or called. She turned and headed toward her sitting area and began making some coffee. She never stopped walking, "lock the door, please". He followed close on her heels. "How do you like your coffee?" He sat down on what was now his favorite chaise and mumbled his likings for the coffee. She handed him the cup of coffee and pulled the Queen Anne straight back chair close to the chaise. He told her everything that happened while sipping the best hotel coffee he ever drunk. She smelled good. She was wearing something citrusy, like she had taken a bath in tropical fruit. Her hair was in disarray, but he had never seen a woman more beautiful. He must have been thinking too long because he heard himself snoring lightly, which woke him up. He looked at her wondering if she knew he had nodded off. "It's been a long time since a man has fallen asleep on me Roxel". He tried standing knowing he needed to head home before he fell dead asleep. His legs were weak from exhaustion and he stumbled. She tried to steady him by grabbing his waist. God, he felt good. He was solid with muscles that ripped for days. 'You are too tired to leave, Roxel. You can sleep on the chaise. I won't tell anyone if you don't tell anyone, she said with a mischievous smirk on her face"

Pharise felt soft like cotton candy, which was one of his favorite things to lick. He could imagine covering her with the sticky confection and licking every sweet place. His mind was wondering again. He would have to focus. He wanted to absolutely turn down her offer, but he couldn't. His legs felt like lead and he remembered he hadn't eaten all day. Obediently, he sat back down and leaned back. "Can I ask you a favor?"

"Yea, they seem to be coming more frequently".

"Pharise, I owe you big time. Is there any way you can order me something to eat from room service? I will forever be in your debt".

Pharise stopped dead in her tracks. "Roxel, am I a friend or an enemy?" Her persistent stare held his gaze.

"Friend," he said as he looked at her through lowered lashes.

"Well, you don't owe me anything. Friends do things for friends. They don't have any hidden agendas. There is no way you can drive and you're starved. Friends are there for each other". She walked away as he watched the sassy sway of her hips. *I like her, he admitted.* She phoned room service, who made another exception given the lateness and brought up soup and a huge club sandwich. He managed to get most of it down before sleep took over. He remembered turning the television on and watched some Bruce Willis movie. That was the last thing he remembered before falling into a deep sleep. She covered him with a blanket that housekeeping brought up along with a couple of pillows. She laughed out loud thinking, this was the most she had entertained in the last two years. She returned to her bed in the other part of the suite and had her best sleep in months. It probably had nothing to do with the good looking man stretched out on her chaise snoring lightly. He brought a sense of security to her life even though she knew that tonight, he had been vulnerable. And, that was her last thought.

Chapter 9

THE ALARM CLOCK screaming in her ear woke her up. She stretched toward her alarm clock and saw 6:30. She was going to be late. She threw the blanket back and balanced herself on the side of the bed trying to remember last night or rather this morning. Her gaze travelled to the chaise where the neatly folded throws occupied the space where Roxel had slept. On top of the blankets was a note. She was disappointed that he didn't wake her to let her know he was leaving. She picked up the note as she headed toward the bathroom to shower. She would have walked straight into the wall if she hadn't smelled coffee. She looked over into the entertaining area and a table was set with breakfast. The sweet aromatic smell of the coffee was her undoing. Her attention drifted back to the note. It simply said,

"Pharise,

Thank you for last night. It was pretty special to me. I have never had a woman who was my friend, a first. You are definitely amazing. I need to ask you for another favor. I would love for you to join me for dinner tomorrow evening. Please don't say no. It seems that I have been monopolizing a lot of your time. I realize that I've been asking a lot from you lately, but afford me the opportunity to do something for you. And, I have kept you up late the last two nights and you will probably be late this morning. My life is pretty complicated right now, but I would love to spend some time getting to know you. I can't guarantee anything, but I would like for this to be a "date". I really like you. See you soon.

P.S. Can we do the sleepover thing again? I knew that would make you smile. Until tomorrow, I mean today.

Roxel"

Pharise was laughing because she hadn't invited Roxel over to her hotel room, yet. That hadn't stopped him from showing up two nights in a row. She figured he was just vulnerable and she was an objective ear from him. She didn't want to be burdened with anyone else's issues. Working through her own problems was her priority. She had to remember that she was on vacation. She would help Roxel find the culprit and then she would be on her way, other than to occasionally send him a Christmas card or something. If she would tell the truth, she liked Roxel, too. She liked everything about him. Last night, she hadn't had a nightmare. She wouldn't go all the way to attribute it to Roxel being a few feet from her bed, but his presence had given her a sense of peace. She had eaten half of the breakfast and drank a cup and a half of coffee by the time she stepped into the shower embracing the hot water. It seemed to be rinsing away all her disappointments, her fears, and her losses. The steamy cocoon was just temporary, but she enjoyed it, none the less.

It was after eight o'clock when she finally arrived at the facility. It was her plan to get an early start interviewing employees. She stopped by Roxel's office to find out where he wanted her to set up. There were a few extra offices at the other end of the hall that would suit her just fine. "Good morning", she said with an eagerness to get to the bottom of things.

"Sorry to have left before you woke, but I needed to check on the employee in the hospital. It probably wouldn't have gone over well for me to wear the same clothes two days in a row" he said with that drop dead gorgeous smile. She hoped the pretty boy wasn't trying to reel her in. It wouldn't work, she hoped.

"I need a space to work. Where can I set up?" Her face appeared relaxed, something that came with a good night's sleep.

"I have the perfect place. It has executive amenities and I think it will provide you with the space necessary to interview employees and to have meetings, if you choose". Before she had an opportunity to reply, the quality manager, Evelyn Cash, entered Roxel's office like she owned the place. Speaking directly to Roxel without the smallest acknowledgment that she was in the room, "I want to move my things in the office next door to you, Roxel." She all but purred. "I'll have the facility workers begin moving it today. Did you need me to find a space for your guests? We can always put them in the back by the shop".

Pharise was about two steps from telling her where she could put her "space". Everyone knew that the shop area was so noisy that couldn't even hear yourself think. Did this woman see Pharise as a threat? Maybe, she belonged to Roxel, but it didn't give her the right to be downright rude. She looked like a throwback from the eighties with too much hair, too much make-up, and her clothes were way too tight. She didn't know what Roxel's taste in women was, but she was surprised that this woman was even in the running. She wasn't an ugly girl by a long shot. She was what one might describe simply as "too much" of everything, therefore making herself unflattering.

Roxel beat her getting Evelyn in check. "Thank you for your suggestion and the offer to assist me in finding Ms. Mallard a space to work, but I have already taken care of that. She will be using the room next to mine. The office that you are in is your assigned office and I don't recall making any changes. I hope that you will cooperate with Ms. Mallard, who is my guest for as long as she is here. And, I'm not certain if you were aware that it is rude to enter someone's office without being asked to enter and without acknowledging those present. I believe I emailed you earlier looking for the statistical analysis on the new robotic prosthetic limb. I still haven't gotten your response, yet Ms. Rose," emphasizing the Ms. So that she would get his subtle indication that they were on a professional and not on a personal level. She might have a thing for Roxel, but it didn't appear that he had a thing for her. Her feelings were wounded. This woman was angry and hurt. It was written all over her face. And if looks could kill, I was a dead woman. It would seem that I had another enemy and I hadn't even been on the property thirty minutes this morning.

Her face told the story. She didn't like what had just transpired one little bit. Obviously, she was a woman who was used to charming men to get what she wanted. Pharise hoped that she wasn't standing in the woman's way. If she and Roxel had a thing, she certainly wouldn't interfere. He wasn't her type.

Roxel helped Pharise get set up in the office by his. The two offices were mirror images of each other and possessed the same amenities. She tried to convince Roxel that a fancy office was not necessary. She would do fine in one of the other, smaller ones. However, he had simply glared at her with narrow eyes and frowns settling in over his brow, "this office is the only one available". She knew that he was not being completely truthful, but she wouldn't push the issue. "Thank you", she said and diverted her attention away from him and started to review all the documents from the recent incidents. She interviewed two employees yesterday and scheduled three more for today. She hadn't realized that he was still in the door until he said, "lunch will be provided for the staff and visitors today. It should be here around 11:30. When there's a lot going on, lunch is brought in as a way of reducing everyone's stress". "Thanks, I appreciate the invite," she said. He nodded and returned to his office and she continued working.

He couldn't figure out what was drawing him to Pharise. Today, she had worn a black pin-striped skirt suit that stopped about two inches above her knee. Her hair was pulled back into some elaborate pony tail that took on a life of its own when she walked. It looked like she was dressed for Wall Street rather than a plant. She was focused on her work. He had faith that she would find the clues needed to isolate those responsible for the accidents. She had been working non-stop interviewing employees, going over incident reports, reviewing photographs, inspecting the machinery and observing the work processes. The union stewards and president had come to him wondering why she was out on the floor so much. After he explained that she, along with some others, was investigating the recent incidents. They asked a few more questions about Pharise's background. He got a funny feeling about the number and kind of questions they were asking, particularly personal questions about Pharise. Maybe, he was becoming a little over-protective towards Pharise. He had assured the union staff that he would keep them up to date with any findings or any new developments.

His thoughts were interrupted when the investigator, Jessie Rice, and his team stopped in his office. "Roxel, we found evidence of tampering on the scissor lift and some other machinery in the plant. I called in some criminal engineers to look at pieces of equipment that may be targeted by the sabotagers. The local police department and the feds have been notified. What I suggest is that you limit the discussion of this information to any of the employees, including your supervisors and staff until we find out who is behind all of this. I have also called in some additional agents, who will work as temporary employees, to be our eyes and ears out on the floor. Although most of the employees here are loyal to a fault, there are some murmurings about robotics eliminating jobs and developing lean processes, which may impact other jobs. Some of the employees were nervous about the company integrating new technology to perform jobs that they have been doing for years. These new ideas may be the catalyst for prompting workers to become edgy. However, I wouldn't think that it would provoke anyone to harm their co-workers, but I wouldn't put it past anyone. Also, I have heard that some female employees have taken issue with you. It seems that you may have a history with a couple of people in upper management that didn't end well. Again, we don't believe this would motivate anyone to hurt someone else, but you never know".

Roxel was about to blow. The audacity of them thinking that a couple of scorned women were the root of the plant's problems was ridiculous. He had taken two women out at this plant in four years; one was a senior manager and the other the quality manager. He had to admit both were gross errors in judgment. Since, he had not been the interim plant manager back then, there wasn't a huge issue. Both he and the senior manager and he had gone to college together and had been friends for years. She had asked him to escort her to a friend's wedding. The woman had wanted more than he was willing to give. He did not want a committed relationship as he had told her on several occasions. She didn't know how to take no for an answer. She thought that his accompanying her to the wedding would change his tune. It hadn't and he said so. She didn't like it. She had never been shy with words and that time was no exception. He hadn't stayed for the wedding and this had dissolved their friendship. She continued to work at the facility because she was a good manager. Since that time, they had learned to be cordial to each other and work together on a professional level.

Technically, he had never dated the quality manager, although she would not have the same recollection of events. The company, including corporate officers, occasionally went out on team building exercises. On one occasion, he invited her to ride with him along with a couple of other employees. She had hung on to him the entire time. He didn't particularly like clingy women. They had gone to a local recreational facility and played pool and played some golf. Every where he moved, she moved. In an effort not to hurt her feelings, he had allowed her some latitude. The other managers had gotten alternate rides back to their vehicles because he needed to settle the bill. Janice had not and on the ride back to her car, she allowed her dress to inch up her thigh. She was a decent looking woman, but he had made it a point not to mix business with pleasure. Anyway, she wasn't his kind of woman. She was too forward and too needy. She had one too many drinks and thought she could take things to the next level. He had told her in no uncertain terms that he was not interested. He was flattered, but that was as far as that would go. She seemed to take it well, but had never stopped trying to change his mind. She was persistent to say the least.

Roxel finally said, "I don't believe that a woman is behind these accidents. That doesn't make sense." He went on to tell them about the two incidents with the women at the plant. He, also, told them about the earlier conversation with the union workers. They reviewed pictures of the equipment that was tampered with and he could see that they were accidents waiting to happen. He shook his head in disbelief. If he hadn't seen it with his own eyes, he would not have believed it. Some crazy person or persons might actually harm someone else because they believed jobs might be cut. This didn't make any sense. They hadn't even planned to cut any jobs. Although the economy had impacted the number of people having surgical procedures, they had still been holding their own as a company. They hadn't laid anyone off and had no intentions of doing so. He didn't know where they were getting their information or why they had felt a need to use criminal tactics. He didn't know how hurting others would benefit them. Jessie said that they would need to determine the motive first. After that, they should be able to narrow down the search. It felt better to have his team around. He knew that his dad would want an update. That would have to wait until he left the office. He invited the men to have lunch with them and they all accepted.

Lunch had been there about thirty minutes, but he hadn't seen any sign of Pharise. He hadn't realized that he was waiting on Pharise before he fixed his plate. He went to her office and she wasn't there. *Where was she?* By this time, she was walking down the hall with John Braxton. He wondered why they were so tight. He wondered if John was her type. He hoped not. He couldn't quite figure out why that would bother him, but it did. Like he said, he would never mix business with pleasure again. However, technically, Pharise didn't work for him, but right now she was working at his company. So, maybe, he would just bide his time and see what happened. She hadn't mentioned whether or not she would accept his dinner invitation. His day had been non-stop so far and he didn't know when he would see the light of day.

Pharise had gone to check on John after she had gotten to a stopping point in her interviews. She had a lot of information and she would probably spend the next couple of days in her hotel reviewing all the documents she had collected. She still wanted to get some sightseeing in. She didn't want to forget that she was on vacation, which was her primary reason for being in Washington, DC. Jessie and the other agents had everything in place and she believed that they would be able to find out who the culprits were soon. She would let them do her job. "Hey, John, how have you been doing?"

"Hey you, come on in. How are things going?"

She knew she could trust John, but didn't know if Roxel wanted those not directly involved in the investigation to be informed about what was going on. "Well, we've been gathering a lot of information. We should have something soon. How's the dating stuff going?" John admitted he had been using the social media to help with dating prospects.

"I got a call from my ex-wife and she told me she's getting married. It's not that I have feelings for her anymore, but it seems to validate that I failed in that part of my life. She was not totally at fault. I abandoned her because of my job and I hate myself for that. I truly did love her, but she said that I didn't love her more than my job. I was too busy climbing the corporate ladder that I failed to see how much I was giving up to get there. Many people would probably say that I have arrived, but when I look around and take inventory—I can tell you that it wasn't quite worth it. I'm not sure why I couldn't see it then. We had a long talk this time. She told me how lonely she always felt in our marriage. She didn't blame me for my ambitions because she said that was one of the things she loved about me. She just couldn't stand to be third in my life behind my job and my ambition. She admitted that she still loved me and always would, but hadn't been in love with me for a very long time. She wanted me to stop paying her alimony and she had even contacted her attorney to have him to contact the courts to do so. It feels like I lost my best friend. She and her new husband are moving to the west coast. The worse thing is that she's pregnant. She always wanted a baby. I kept asking her to wait until I got through one project and then another. Eventually, she stopped asking".

"John, she's moved on with her life and it's time for you to do the same. Things don't always work out the way we plan. And, if I know you, you will do it way better the next time. You apologized and she accepted your apology. That released both of you to go forward with living your lives. I wish that we could go back in time and redo our mistakes, but we can't. If I had the chance to go back, I would be sure to tell my mother how much I needed for her to live. I would ask her for the family recipes for the chow chow and the sweet potato pies. I would ask for all of the family secrets and I would have been sure that I told her I loved her so much a million times, but I can't go back. I wish I could." I could feel the pressure from the tears welling up at the back of my eyes. I took a tissue from his desk and dried my eyes. "John, we're going make it through this. It's going to be hard, but we'll make it through. Let's go get some lunch. Roxel said that he was ordering lunch for the staff".

"Good." He put his game face on and came from around his desk. "What are you doing for dinner tonight? Let's go hang out at Julie's, a local soul food restaurant that has an uptown flair." She hadn't forgotten about Roxel's invitation, but she wasn't ready for anything serious. She and Roxel needed to sit down and have a discussion so that neither one of them would get the wrong impression of things. She would ask Roxel for a rain check.

"Sure, I'll meet you there at six-thirty. I have a couple of errands to run."

They walked down the hall together and continued a light conversation. When they reached the conference room, where lunch had been set-up, she looked up into Roxel's face. Although she couldn't quite make out his mood, she knew he was unhappy about something. That point was hammered home when she smiled at him and he failed to return one. Oh well, she thought, he was in one of his moods again. He really did need to get that thorn out of his butt. She was certain she hadn't done anything.

43

If he wanted her to know what was wrong with him, she would leave it to him to tell her. If he didn't, so be it. The food looked divine. She and John fixed their plates and took a seat at the executive table. Roxel sat at the opposite end engaged in conversation with some employees. On occasion, they would both look up and their eyes would meet and one or both of them would divert their gaze. There couldn't be two more stubborn people. They were like oil and vinegar, they would never mix.

John could tell that Roxel was interested in his friend, Pharise. By the look on his face, he was pissed off at one or both of them. He had never goaded a man about a woman. Unless Roxel asked him if he was interested in Pharise, he wouldn't offer that information. Roxel Stapleton had, indeed, met his match.

Pharise stopped by Roxel's office to let him know that she would not be in for the next couple of days and to tell him why. And, she asked for a rain check on dinner. There was no sense in asking why he had an attitude with her. "You can e-mail me with any updates and I will do the same". He stared at her as if she spoke another language. "What?" she all but yelled.

Roxel's asked, "Is there something going on between you and John?"

"That's none of your business. If you have a problem with me being friends with other employees then that's your problem, not mine. I will not be able to go to dinner with you tonight. John is my friend and that is all that I will say about that."

He could tell that she was livid. Her eyes had narrowed so that she looked oriental and her mouth had thinned almost to a single line. Roxel reached for the self control that always seemed to escape him where Pharise was concerned. "I'm sorry; I'm not sure why I asked you that. Like I said, I like you and I was out of line."

She didn't open her mouth. She just continued glaring at him with her head held at a slightly tilted angle. She was turning to walk out of his office when Roxel blurted out, "what are you doing tomorrow? Will you go out to dinner with me then?" He wasn't too proud to beg.

"I'll let you know", she said. She turned and walked out the office. He turned his chair around to see her walking towards her car. He stood and continued watching her get in and pull off. Roxel continued to watch as she exited the premises. Another dark sedan pulled out slowly behind her. He never would have noticed, but he thought it was a little odd that two men would be sitting in a parked car in the salaried parking lot. Roxel knew all of the salaried staff's cars and had never seen this car before. He took a mental note of the license plate and jotted it down as he settled back in his chair. He could tell it was going to be a long day. Before he got too engrossed in all the work he had pending on his desk, he needed to check with security about the questionable dark sedan. Security stated they had wondered about the car, too. The car didn't enter through security. The owner must have had a proxy card which allowed them entry and only employees had those. The security guard stated she had not been there that morning when they came in, but would follow up tomorrow to determine the identity of the driver.

Chapter 10

"I WANT Ms. MALLARD to understand the consequences of snooping into things that are none of her business. It is evident that Roxel will listen to any recommendations she makes. Jobs are at stakes. And, no one will lose their job on my watch. Our workers need those extra hours to survive. They are depending on me to make sure that they don't lose any money with all these changes. Her being in the plant poses a big problem and it is causing me money. That's why the accidents have to happen. Roxel doesn't get it, but he will." *His voice was hoarse burned by his mostly liquid diet of gin and juice.* "If you can't take care of this problem, then I will get someone else to do it. Then, I'll get someone to take care of you, too. I hope we understand each other." The two men staked out in the dark sedan had their boss on speaker phone. Things had been heating up at the plant. They had almost gotten caught removing guards off some equipment. They had chosen to sabotage equipment in places where it would be the least visible. Up until now, they had been pretty successful. Their luck might be running out. Ms. Mallard had been taking pictures of some of the equipment and had identified some that they had tampered with. The boss wanted to scare her. So, they would do just that. Maybe then, she would crawl back under whatever rock she had emerged. Then, things at the plant would be forced to go back to the way they were before Roxel came with all his bright ideas on how to make things better. "Yes, boss. We'll make it happen." "I'm glad that you see things my way". He disconnected the non-traceable phone. He had grown to detest the man who owned the voice that had just ended the call. He wondered when he had become a "thug". Initially, he had done little jobs to make a little extra income. His partner was a real thug, who had been in and out of juvenile when he was younger. Now, he was known as a hustler and he wasn't even real good at that. After this job, he would perform a disappearing act and go somewhere and start fresh. He hoped that it wasn't too late. "Hey man, look. Here, she comes and she's alone". He simply nodded his head. He sure hated to mess up her rental. It was a real nice piece of metal. He really liked the late model black Cadillac SUV hybrid. *Oh, well. A job was a job.*

Pharise noticed the sedan pull out behind her and was now following her. The car seemed to be about a fourth of a mile back. This was a rural part of town leading into the city. The fluorescent street lighting seemed to cast a shadow over everything. Pharise had a weird feeling that whoever was following her was up to no good. She had Jessie on speed dial and was waiting on him to answer. The car continued to keep its distance, but now a light rain had begun. Jessie answered on the fourth ring. She told him her fears about the car that appeared to be following her when she heard a loud crash. She screamed into the phone. Her car had been rammed from the back and was now being pushed forward. Her feet were on the brakes and they were down as far as they could go. She heard the tires shrieking and her heart pumping. Her SUV continued to forge forward. She was holding her breath. Her skin felt hot and cold. She would not panic. She remembered passing this way while traveling back and forth to and from the facility. The pushing motion stopped and she could hear Jessie on the other end of the telephone. She had told him where she was and she prayed that he was on his way. The car rear ended her a second time. She heard glass shattering and she knew she had been hit by something. There was no way she wouldn't panic. She held onto the steering wheel as tight as she could. And then everything started spinning as her car left the road and flipped over and over and landed on the driver's side and then there was an annoying silence. Her body was jammed toward her door with gravity causing her body to take the brunt of her own weight. The air bag had exploded in her face emitting suffocating fumes. She smelled smoke and prayed to God that nothing was burning. She heard car doors slam. She felt pain everywhere, but forced herself not to move. She tried not to move, not to breathe. She was partially suspended in air by her seat belt.

"Is she dead?" "I don't know. We didn't have orders to kill her. Why did you hit her car the second time? MK is going to be mad."

"Well, that doesn't matter to me as long as I get my money. He promised 5K's for this job per person. I need mine. I got people I owe breathing down my neck." "Let's get out of here before someone comes".

Pharise tried several times to unbuckle the seat belt with no success. If she could just reach her purse, then she could get the small pocket knife she always kept with her. She could feel the warm liquid running down her face and side, almost blinding her. She knew it was blood. Her telephone could be anywhere. She remembered talking to Jessie on it before they smashed into the back of the rental. She remembered the phone hitting the windshield along with her head. She could feel her purse on the floor under her feet. She used her feet to maneuver it so that she could grab onto the strap. It took three cuts with the blunt knife to release her from the seatbelt which had held her hostage, but it had, also, probably saved her life. The pain seemed to increase in her head and her shoulder. Her mouth felt like cotton. The car was still running and she was able to let down the passenger window. She prayed that she would be able to crawl out. She took the key from ignition. She climbed across the seat. It didn't seem like her limbs wanted to cooperate. The SUV was lying on its side. She pulled herself up and out onto a muddy embankment. It was at least four feet. She had to get her leverage by standing on the passenger side of the truck and grabbed the brush and limbs that surrounded her. The tree limbs bit into her skin. Right now, she was glad she hadn't gotten her nails done because she would have popped every one of them off. Her nails were filled with mud and she had to lose the pumps. She didn't know how long it took her to get on top of the embankment, but she made it. That was the last thing she remembered before losing consciousness.

Jessie wasted no time getting out of the building and following the route Pharise took on a daily basis. Two agents were riding with him. He updated Roxel on the way out the door. Roxel had been worried and had already contacted security about the suspicious car. He was following in his vehicle right behind Jessie. Jessie had mobilized a team quickly to find Pharise, which included John who had overheard him telling Roxel. They hadn't wanted to tell too many people at the plant. They still didn't know who could be trusted. There were four cars following him and he had already contacted the local police and federal agents because this involved some federal issues. His heart was pounding and he could feel the sweat on his forehead. He knew she couldn't have gotten far. He had his high beams on to illuminate the surrounding blackness. They were at a disadvantage because of the darkness and it was still drizzling. He slowed down. He could see muddy car tracks on the side of the road. "God, I hoped she is not down in the embankment". He barely put the car in park before he rushed from his car.

Roxel had made it from his car and to the same point on the landing at the same time as Jessie did. They bent to see what looked like a vehicle. Roxel said, "That's her car. I'm going down there." The SUV was on its side.

Everyone else had gotten out of their cars and was standing at the edge of the drop-off. Jessie stopped a second to survey the area densely populated with trees. His instincts were telling him something. He performed a visual and then he saw what appeared to be a person faced down in the mud on the other side. "I believe that's her, pointing in her direction". Jessie, yelled her name, but saw no movement. He didn't know if her vehicle was stable enough for them to stand on and climb back up to the other side. One of the agents was on the phone getting a helicopter in. There was enough of a clearing to land on the other side. They didn't know how badly she was hurt, so they couldn't afford to waste time.

Jessie tried to convince Roxel and John to stay behind, while he and a couple of the agents tried to reach her. It was easier convincing John than Roxel. Roxel wasn't going to cooperate. "Be careful, the car may not be stable. Roxel nodded, but didn't speak. It felt like all moisture had left his mouth, leaving his lips glued together. It was wet, which meant that they probably wouldn't get good traction. They were able to make it from one side to the other without incident. It was a muddy trek, but they reached her practically all at the same time. She was breathing faintly. The helicopter would be there in a few moments. He simply whispered, "Pharise, hold on." And then, he spoke to God on her behalf.

Roxel could not believe that this was happening. It seemed so surreal. Someone tried to kill Pharise and he was certain this was related to the other incidents at the plant. He was greatly affected by each incident, especially when employees had been hurt. However, this was personal. Somehow, he and Pharise had connected and now she was hanging onto life by a thin thread because some lunatic with an agenda believed she was expendable. Well she wasn't. He phoned his father and explained what was going on. John would call his father back and update him. John might like Pharise, but Roxel was going to convince her that he needed her. There was no way he would let her die, not like this.

They didn't want to move her, but they needed to get her face turned where she could get some air. She was covered in mud and it was hard to see where she was bleeding. A large gash stretched across her hair line. "Pharise, honey, just hold on. You're going to be fine. Can you hear me?" He continued to touch her and held her hand. Somehow, he needed to touch her. He prayed more tonight than he had ever prayed in his life. He repeated the childhood prayers that he had long ago abandoned. Tonight, they needed a miracle.

They heard the soft murmuring in the distance of the helicopter approaching. By then, there were police officers and agents everywhere with their marked and unmarked cars covering the grassy area. They stretched the yellow tape to enclose the area. Jessie instructed everyone to stand back except Roxel and him. The helicopter landed about a hundred feet away in the clearing. Dust and tree limbs were thrown everywhere. The lights from the helicopter illuminated the entire area. The emergency personnel exited the helicopter with a transfer board. They turned her with one fluid motion to her back. They told us they would start the IV once they got back inside. They took her blood pressure and pulse; both were on the low side of normal. Their faces appeared grim. She was being transported to the same trauma hospital that he had been with the last employee. They lifted her and got her inside the helicopter safely. All of us stood there watching the helicopter. The plane remained in that spot for a few more minutes while they continued to work on her. Then, without warning, it lifted off heading towards the hospital.

The agents that came with Jessie were busy surveying the area for clues. They were looking at tire tracks, taking pictures, and taking measurements. A wrecker had arrived on the scene and it looked like something from LA Law. Jessie said that he would stay to supervise everything there. He knew Roxel would keep him updated. John had informed Roxel's family Pharise had been found. He was a longtime family friend that knew that I was overwhelmed at all that had taken place. His eyes met mine. "Roxel, she's going to be fine." A few seconds lapsed when he said, "we're not involved, but we are good friends. I don't want her hurt. I'm giving you fair warning".

Roxel couldn't remember the last time someone had threatened him and gotten away with it, but he understood what he was saying. "It's not my intention to hurt her. Beyond that, I don't have any answers". With that, Roxel turned and headed towards his car and they both headed to the hospital.

Chapter 11

H E HATED USING HIRELINGS for his jobs. They were usually too incompetent, like these two. He didn't want anyone killed because he didn't welcome that kind of "heat". He wanted Pharise Mallard to abandon her mission to determine the source of the incidents. She was getting too close and he wanted her out of the facility. She had been seen taking pictures of some equipment that his guys had been prepping for another accident. Roxel Stapleton didn't know who he was messing with and he needed to make him aware of it. Every new process that they implemented would eventually cause a reduction in overtime hours and ultimately a reduction in employees. Many of the workers needed those extra hours to survive. And, they looked to him for answers to their problems. He knew that these strong armed tactics would only delay the inevitable. The unstable economy was really the root of the problem. If companies wanted to survive these turbulent times, then they would have to make some changes. Some of the changes would not benefit the workers, but they would help the company remain viable. It was during these times that he disliked what he did. In another life, he would have never staged these accidents and allowed the employees, who he worked for, to get hurt. That was before he had a million dollar mortgage, luxury cars, gambling debt, and two ex-wives. The two idiots would land all of them in jail, but he wouldn't go down without a fight. If Ms. Mallard died, then he would hold them responsible. He believed in an "eye for an eye", vengeance would be his to dispense accordingly. One of them would pay with their life and he would gladly pull the trigger to put either or both out of their misery.

Roxel headed for the emergency room's automatic doors in an up-tempo jog with John close behind him. His heart was racing and his palms were sweaty. As the doors closed behind them, they were surrounded by his family, some staff members, and friends. He saw a reassuring look on his mother's face letting him know that everything would work out fine. He had never seen his father look so haggard before. His father, Howard, was sixty-two with dark hair sprinkled with gray. His bronze skin clashed with his mother's fair olive complexion. They were a handsome couple who had taken parenting seriously. His mother was an administrator at a local hospital. Both of his parents retired early so that they could enjoy the fruit of their labor. His dad reached him while holding his gaze and grabbed him in a soulful hug which spoke volumes. His dad, a man of few words, was silently communicating to him that he understood and did not blame him. She had been admitted to the ER and was now in a suite being assessed by doctors. "Son, they are going to take a lot of tests on her to make sure nothing is broken and that she doesn't have any internal injuries. It may be awhile before we hear anything", his mother said. "I have spoken to your investigator and they have photographs of the suspect's car that are pretty clear. The images of the two perpetrators were not that clear, but he believed that they would be able to refine the images to identify them. Technology, today, is amazing. We will get to the bottom of this. Jessie, also, mentioned that they had installed security cameras throughout the facility and had gotten some real interesting images. They would continue to check the recently classified cameras that were the latest in surveillance technology. One thing that was clear, the union workers were involved in one way or another. "Roxel, we are going to find who did this and make them pay".

Roxel was still on auto pilot with adrenalin to spare. He greeted his brother and sister who never failed to support him. His brother had returned from the cafeteria with coffee for everyone. John and his dad were old friends and they took a chair engrossed in a deep conversation. He felt like he was going to lose it if he didn't get some information soon. Before he left the hospital, he was sure he would have no sole left on his shoes. His brother jokingly told him that he needed some Ritalin or something to take the edge off. Yea, he did. But the only thing that would help him was to know that she was alright. Until then, he would be a nervous wreck.

There was something about her that pulled at him. As far as he could remember, he had never dated a woman that resembled her in the least. Usually he dated women who were paper thin, attractive, fair skinned daughters of the elite. They all seemed to be the debutante type. He knew he never set out to choose women like this, but that's who he usually ended up dating. These women were great conversationalist and very accommodating. They never put up too much of a fuss if he had to cancel a date, reschedule, or if he broke things off because they weren't a good fit for him. The more he thought about it, the more he realized that they were more like business arrangements. That's probably why it had been months since he last had a real date. He wouldn't say that these women were boring. However, they weren't that exciting either. Most of them were the educated type who pursued becoming the perfect wife and mother. He didn't know enough about Pharise to say whether she wanted to be a mother or a wife. One thing he could say with certainty was that Pharise was not boring and he doubted that there would ever be a dull moment with her around. Pharise didn't look like the model type. Oh, she was drop dead gorgeous and she had a curvy luscious frame. There was no logical reason for him to pursue her, but he would. He had no intention of failing. His future depended on it. First, Pharise had to come through this alright. She just had to make it.

The attending physician came to the waiting room and called for their family. He instantly recognized the tall statuesque man as Dr. Harold Stanton, a friend of his parents. After they all greeted each other, he invited everyone back to her room. "You have quite an entourage traveling with you today. Ms. Mallard must be quite special to you all." They all agreed, but Roxel could feel all eyes on him. "She looks worse than she is. We had the nurses to help clean her up so she would be a little more presentable. It looks like her head hit the windshield. She has a nice gash along her hair line and a concussion. We stitched the gash up. It took us a long time to get all of the pieces of glass out. She has a lot of small cuts and abrasions. She also banged her right shoulder up and has a lot of bruising and a small hematoma. Her hands and knees are scraped from crawling out of the car. She lost a moderate amount of blood and we gave her two units of blood. We've given her some pain medicine to make her comfortable. The MRI's and x-rays indicated she had no broken bones or internal injuries. She had lots of scrapes and bruises. She's had a heck of a day."

We all entered her room, filling it to capacity. We stood back to give the staff room to work. Her face was black and blue and the puckered stitches were tattooed on her head. One eye was a little puffy and closed. She was trying to look at us out of the other one and it appeared that it was difficult for her to focus. Gravity pulled me toward her and I searched for her hand to hold. "It's going to be alright, Pharise." His other hand reached up to her face and smoothed her hair back.

"Hey, I guess I wasn't careful enough." She grimaced and tried to reposition herself in the bed. "Do you need something for pain?" He asked. Pharise struggled to reposition herself in bed and said, "No, I just needed to get off my right side."

In no time flat, she was talking to everyone and answering questions. She was introduced to all my family and she easily won them over with her cheerful disposition, in spite of her present predicament. Pharise said, "Somebody, hand me a mirror." Silence filled the room and nobody moved.

"Pharise, why don't you wait a while? You got pretty banged up." She rolled her eyes at me.

"Really?" she said. "I think I know that better than anyone. Find me a mirror Roxel. I want to see how I look." Panic was evident on the faces in the room.

My mother pillaged through her purse and presented her with a compact. "Pharise, right now you probably don't look your best, but we can all tell that you are quite lovely. The nurses are going to give you some instructions on how to reduce the swelling and the bruises will begin fading in a few days. Don't get discouraged by what you see in the mirror. The body is miraculous and the healing process has already started." If you didn't know it, one would have thought that my mother, Mrs. Tristan Stapleton, was Pharise's mother as they spoke to each other.

However, all Pharise heard was "blah, blah, blah".

Pharise liked Roxel's mom, even though her son knew how to and did push her buttons. She remembered that she had walked out of his office totally pissed at him. He spoke before he thought. His arrogance amazed her. He had no right to ask her about her and John's relationship unless he was interested. *Was he interested? Did she really want him to be interested?* That was a question that she would not dwell on. However, she had to admit that Roxel was also very caring and had gone out of his way to make sure she was comfortable at the facility. She liked Roxel, but he was on a totally different level on the "food chain". His passion for things seemed to connect them.

While opening the mirror she looked into Roxel's dark brown eyes and then she glanced down at the compact. The image looking back at her was unfamiliar and terrifying. Her face was all swollen with dried blood stains all along the stitches on her hair line. Her right eye was huge and there were black and blue bruises on her forehead. Her lip was slightly cut. She looked horrible. She felt alone, even though the room was filled with people who cared. The one person who she wanted to be there was not, her mom. Her mom had died as a result of the injuries related to a horrible car wreck. And now, a car wreck had almost taken her life. She felt tears filling the back of her eyes and tried with all of her might to prevent them from falling. She glanced at the image again. It was then that she felt the tears running down her face. She took her hand to swipe them away, but they kept coming. Roxel's mom reached out and hugged her and the dam broke. She could not contain her emotions. Pharise would often think of her mom and shed a few tears, but she had never allowed herself to have a good cry. She hadn't realized that Roxel and his mom had traded places until she realized she was leaning into a brick hard chest. The tears slowed and she wondered if they all thought she was having some type of nervous breakdown or something. Roxel was wiping her face in a gentle loving way.

Dr. Stanton returned to the room, after being called away to handle another emergency. "I know you want to be discharged tonight, but it is not in your best interest to be alone because of the concussion. We can admit you and keep you here a couple of days at least, so that you can receive the care and the observation that you need. If you had family here, I would consider letting you go if I could be guaranteed you wouldn't be alone and that you would get the rest necessary for you to heal. I have, also, prescribed some pain relievers, antibiotics, and muscle relaxers. The nurse will give you a tetanus shot before you are discharged." The doctor hoped that he was not the cause of the tears that dampened her face. "Please, if you discharge me, I promise I'll be ok."

The doctor shook his head from side to side. "I'm sorry, Pharise. There are too many things that could go wrong with a closed head injury."

"She can stay at my home for the next few days. I'll make sure that she is observed, takes her medicine and gets the rest she needs." He looked at his mother soliciting her help. "My mother can assist me in getting her all the things she needs."

Everyone turned and looked at Roxel as if he had a third eye. He wasn't sure why he had offered to take a woman into his home and take care of her. This certainly was a first for him. He knew he was asking for trouble. The way he saw it she didn't have much of a choice. She could remain in the hospital for the next few days in a boring sterile environment or she could hang out with him, receive the pampering of a lifetime, and enjoy delicious meals. He didn't know how anyone could refuse an offer like this one, but when he looked into her eyes, he saw doubt and mistrust.

As much as she wanted to refuse his offer, she wanted to get out of the hospital more. The place gave her the creeps. Hospitals brought too many painful memories. "Pharise, as much as my son is a pain in the behind, he is more of a gentleman. I assure you that he will take good care of you. I will stop by and check on you to see if you need something. He's almost a better cook than me." She could tell that his mother adored him and the rest of her family.

"I don't want to be a burden on anyone and besides he has a company to run."

Roxel's father spoke, "He needs to take a few days off. The investigation is coming along. I'm sure that we will find those responsible soon. Security cameras were installed throughout the facility. I'll keep an eye on things for a few days until he gets back."

The word "no" was on the tip of her tongue. Instead, she heard herself agreeing to stay with Roxel for a few days until she could get back on her feet.

Pharise was overwhelmed by the smile that dominated his face and he mouthed, "thank you."

Pharise felt she was way out of her league. She didn't believe for one moment that he was interested in her romantically. Apparently, he felt sorry for her. She was alone in a big city. Pharise had never stayed in the same house as a man before, but anything was better than being cooped up in a hospital. She received hugs and well wishes from John, Roxel's family and a couple of employees from Allegory. It felt great that she wasn't alone during this ordeal. Mrs. Stapleton helped her get dressed as they waited on the discharge papers. The pain medicine kept her off-balanced and groggy. Her vacation had taken an interesting turn.

Chapter 12

ROXEL DROPPED OFF her prescriptions on the way home. He would get her settled in and get his house keeper to pick up the medicines, as well as the other things a woman might need. She had given his mom a list of things to bring from her hotel room. He expected his mother to bring things over later that night. Roxel lifted Pharise from the car with ease. She wasn't thin, but she wasn't big either. She curled her arms around his neck and leaned her soft body into his. Her lush body felt heavenly, better than any woman he had ever held. She was dreaming. It didn't seem like a pleasant one. He picked up his pace, disarmed the alarm and headed toward the largest guest bedroom. He removed her shoes and jacket. He pulled a throw over her. His mother would bring some clothes for her to change into later.

The plan was to prepare them something to eat. It had been a long day and he, like most people, wasn't a fan of hospital food. He planned to cook something light when the ringing of the doorbell interrupted his thoughts. His mother and house keeper arrived simultaneously. His mother unpacked her luggage. "I brought dinner from your favorite Italian restaurant. I need you to get it out the car." She had brought enough food it seemed to feed a small army. He unloaded her car and assisted the housekeeper unloading hers. The house keeper had brought enough groceries for a week. He had told her that he wouldn't need her for a few days and suggested that she could go to Virginia to see her children. He would pay for the cost of the trip and her weekly wages. She was like a second mother to him and he knew she had been longing to see her grandchildren. This would be the perfect opportunity.

He kissed his mother as she passed him going to the guest room. His mother said, "She needs to wake up to eat and take her medicine before the pain returns. "I'll help her dress for bed. Set the table and put the food out. We'll be out shortly."

His mother and Pharise entered the kitchen about fifteen minutes later. He had placed the food in a warmer, not knowing how long they would take. He asked the housekeeper to have dinner with them. He believed that Pharise would enjoy the company of the women and he hoped that it would help her settle in.

Dinner had been delicious and he had welcomed the company of his mother and housekeeper, who left moments earlier. Pharise was back in bed and he busied himself cleaning the kitchen and putting up the leftovers. Before he retired to bed, he stopped by the room to make sure Pharise didn't need anything. He knocked gently on the door and heard no response. He quietly opened the door and saw her lying on her side with a rhythmic rise and fall of her chest. He could see the top of her breast in the light lacy gown. He stood there ogling her. Something must be wrong with him. She had pulled her hair back in a pony tail and her face was free of make-up. He moved closer to her and pulled up the blanket over her. She was having another dream. He wasn't quite sure whether she was having a nightmare. His sister had decorated this room and placed a rocker and ottoman set in the corner near a framed bay window. He didn't know why, but he took a seat in the rocker. He removed his shoes and tie. He placed the golden cuff links on a night table and unbuttoned his short. He reached for the extra throw on the edge of her bed and leaned back in the chair.

Pharise was having another nightmare. Lately, she dreaded sleep. That was probably why she had basically become an insomniac. She was being chased again. No matter how fast she drove, they still followed. So, she drove as fast as she could, cut in and out of traffic. People were honking their horns, but she couldn't be concerned with them. She didn't have a clue where she was going. The city was unfamiliar. Her heart was beating so fast that she could hear the sounds resonating through her clothes. It seemed that her car was going slower and slower and they increased their speed. She watched their rapid approach in her mirror. She screamed, but nothing came out. Was this the end?

Pharise did not seem like an intruder in his home. It felt like she belonged there. He was awakened by a blood curdling cry. She was shaking and sobbing and talking out of her head. He gently grabbed her shoulders,

"Wake up Pharise, wake up". She became more hysterical and he was forced to shake her harder. "Wake up". Her eyes opened and instantly she sat up and held on to me for dear life. "Shh, what's wrong?" Her breathing came in quick shallow short breaths. His sister had panic attacks when she was younger and he knew what needed to be done to pull her out of this. He raced to the kitchen to retrieve a paper bag, only leaving her for a moment. "Pharise, breathe in the bag. You need to take deep breaths. Concentrate on breathing in and out." He kept rubbing her back in a circular motion to calm her down. The side of her face was smashed to my chest as she continued to cry. Her body shivered against his. She was holding on to him for dear life, as if she needed him. Roxel wanted her to need him. She quieted down. "Do you want to talk about it?"

"I can't," she whispered.

"That's fine." He lay back on the pillow taking her with him with her head on his chest. His hands roamed across her back and her face. Her breathing evened out and she drifted back to sleep. He was soon overtaken by sleep, himself.

He felt her stir around three in the morning. She was a restless sleeper; even now her leg was thrown across his. His blood felt like molten lava. He had never survived temptation so sweet. He pushed the runaway strands of hair from her face. She opened her eyes to stare at him like she had never seen him before. She touched his face ever so gently. She could feel his unshaven face. He'd slept in his slacks, afraid to leave her alone and afraid that his desire for her would overshadow his need to take care of her. She felt like a voyeur on an adventure of a lifetime. She traced his lips with her finger and she felt his breathing change. His eyes bore into hers warning her not to go too far. She wanted to taste his lips. She raised her head and her mouth gently grazed his. He allowed her to explore his body without censure. She pressed her mouth more firmly on his, silently requesting entry and he obliged her. He allowed her to control of the kiss this time. If he were rational, he would stop her. She was vulnerable right now and he knew this was the last thing she needed, but she felt so good. She palmed his chest allowing her hands to become brazen. Her kiss was sweet and therapeutic, healing the ghost of his past. He took control of the kiss. His body was no longer able to resist the passion that he had been controlling.

She was grinding her pelvis into his groin. The heat from their bodies was enough to cause them to spontaneously combust.

A ringing telephone interrupted them. "Is that my phone," she asked. Her raspy voice sounded foreign to her own ears. Roxel reached beside the bed and retrieved her purse from the antique night stand. She attempted to free herself from his embrace to no avail. His eyes were closed and his hand snugly hugged her waist. He had contacted her family last night along with her boss, Jason. It was obvious that her family was close. Her sister had threatened to be on the next plane heading to Washington unless he came completely clean regarding the events that had led to her sister being run off the road. After he assured Felice that Pharise was being taken care of and that she had no broken bones, she calmed down some. There was little doubt that her sister wasn't totally convinced that she didn't need to still get on that plane. Roxel agreed to contact her daily to give her updates. This was the only thing that appeased her. He would make sure that he kept his word. Her sister assured him that she would contact their brother and let him know what happened. Felice admitted that their brother, Trey, was not as easy going as she and that she wouldn't put it past him to show up in Washington.

Pharise spoke to Jason on the phone. "Jason, I'm fine. I got banged up a little when the car rolled into the ditch. I look much worse than I feel. My face looks like someone hit it with a bat. I don't know if all the swelling is a result of my hitting the windshield or the after effects of me climbing out the ditch. I'll be good as new in a few days. Hopefully, we can find the maniacs who tried to kill me." She felt Roxel's body tense and his embrace tighten. His eyes were closed, but she could tell he wasn't asleep. She heard what Jason was saying, but couldn't believe it.

"Pharise, you are not to continue on this case. The information that you have already gathered has proven to be invaluable. Jessie has looked at some of the photos and he is certain that the perpetrators are present on one of the snapshots. It seems that they were in the process of staging another accident. I need you to take your much needed vacation. Go to the Smithsonian, visit the memorials, or go shopping, but do not return to the facility."

"Why are you doing this? I need closure and I need to find out who the culprits are that want me out of the way. It's not fair for you to take me off this case."

Jason knew that she didn't like being removed from this case, but there was no other way. She was only there to clear the names of the company and not to get killed. She was about as stubborn as they came and he knew she wouldn't concede without a fight. He loved Pharise like a daughter. Although she was motivated to do a good job and had already done an outstanding one up to this point, there was no way he would jeopardize her safety. She would just have to be angry with him. The two of them had been here before and she would eventually get over it. "Pharise, you are no longer working on the Allegory Medical case. You may remain in Washington as long as you like to get some well deserved rest and relaxation. I don't want to fight with you about this, but I will. If you disobey me, I will terminate your employment. I hope that we understand each other."

Pharise ranted and raved, but she knew it wouldn't do any good. She pulled herself away from Roxel and was now pacing the room like a caged animal.

"Pharise, get yourself better. I don't want you to lose it. You have a lot going on right now. If you are to continue being my go-to person, then I need you healthy, physically and emotionally."

Jason was wrong. She knew he was trying to look out for her. More than that, there was no use arguing with him. "Whatever, Jason" and she disconnected the phone.

Jason stared at the phone in his hands for a few minutes while listening to a dial tone sounding in his ear. He had spoken to Roxel last night, who had shared his concerns about Pharise returning to the facility until the perpetrators were behind bars. He failed to share this with Pharise, but when she found out, there would be hell to pay. Roxel might not know it, but his trouble had just started.

It was still early and Pharise needed to go back to bed. He couldn't figure why Jason had called them at five in the morning. He knew she would be wound up. He, also, knew that he would have to pay for broaching the subject with Jason of her not returning to the plant. He didn't know if Jason had shared that bit of information with her, but he knew she would eventually find out. She didn't appear to take things very easily when she felt betrayed. He would deal with her temper if it meant keeping her safe. He walked back in the bedroom. There was no light and he could see the outline of her body nestled under the comfortable. He had showered while she conversed with Jason. He had checked his voice mail and had returned some e-mails. He was, also, on an unofficial vacation. If she let him, he would show her a good time and offer his services as a tour guide. If she didn't, then he would stalk her to make sure she was protected, either way. She was not getting rid of him.

He slid under the cool sheets with her. He prayed that she still wanted him close in the bed with her. He had never been presumptuous, but he was bordering on it today. "If you want to sleep alone, I'll understand. You had a nightmare earlier and I didn't want you to be alone." He waited. *Maybe she had fallen asleep.*

"Did you know that Jason wasn't going to let me to go back in the plant?"

It would be easy to lie to her and remain in her good grace, but he had never been good at lying. And, it was no way to lay a foundation for any kind of relationship. He sighed heavily, "yes, I knew". That was all the information he would give, unless she asked for more. He waited patiently for her to go off on him. She didn't move or say anything. He thought he heard a sniffle, but couldn't be sure. He reached over to hold her.

"Don't. I don't want you to touch me, but you don't have to leave the bed."

Those words had been uttered so quietly that he would have missed them if he had not been listening closely. She had given him permission to remain in bed with her, but he couldn't touch her, nor could he comfort her to erase all the bad things that had happened. He wished that she would have cursed him out or gotten mad and slapped him. His heart was breaking for her, a woman who didn't back down from a fight. Tonight, he wouldn't get much sleep. Not being able to touch her was the worse punishment that he could have been given. However, he would gladly endure his punishment as long as she didn't banish him from her life. He had to admit to himself that Pharise Mallard was his correct change. He hoped fate would be on his side.

Pharise had a gigantic headache from the screaming match with Jason. Jason thought that he could control her life by threatening to fire her. She knew he was worried about her. If she was truthful, she was a little worried, too. She was worried, but that didn't translate into being afraid. She was more disappointed with Roxel than angry with him. He and Jason had conspired against her to keep her away from doing her job. And she was not alright with that. He should have just asked her. She wasn't sure her response would have been favorable, but at least it would have allowed them the space to talk through it. What she needed most was a friend and not Roxel's controlling attitude. There was no place in her life for people who desired to control her. Her father had tried his hand at controlling her and it didn't work then and it wouldn't work now. They were intensely attracted to each other. Would the attraction be enough to hold the fragile thread that bound them together from breaking?

They danced around each other for the next few days being cordial, but the tension had become insurmountable. Roxel made certain that she was comfortable in his home. It was evident that he was a trust fund baby. His home was magazine worthy. Cozy fireplaces were in the great room and the bedrooms. The bay windows stretched from the ceiling to the floors in most rooms with track lighting strategically placed throughout the house giving it ample lighting. The kitchen looked like it belonged on the Food Network channel. There were stainless steel appliances, two double ovens. She loved his house, but there was something missing. She couldn't quite put her finger on it. "Oh well, that's not my problem anyway," she mused.

Pharise contacted the emergency room doctor a couple of days ago to make a follow-up appointment. Her appointment was at two this afternoon. Anticipation of being cleared to return to her hotel and getting on with her vacation caused her to complete her morning routine in half the time. Roxel had said he would be ready to leave at one. She would eternally be indebted to him for taking good care of her. His mother had been a jewel, too. Roxel and she had not done much talking lately. She missed that. She packed all of her things, either way she didn't plan to return to Roxel's home. If the doctor wouldn't release her, she would crash at John's place until she was cleared. She hadn't discussed this with Roxel for fear that he would try to change her mind. That wasn't going to happen. *"He should be happy to get rid of me and get on with his life."* She knew she was the reason he hadn't been back to the plant, but she would remedy that.

He was bringing the mail in, while waiting on her to come down stairs. He wanted to make sure they had plenty of time to get to the appointment. He was reading an advertisement when he sensed she was on the stairs. Today, she wore an intoxicating scent that was a sensual magnet that reeled him in. She wore black capris pants with a multi-colored international blouse that boasted of a rounded neck and an Indian appeal. She was wearing eye make-up today with shades of bronze, gold, and green that were blended well to make her look more exotic than usual. The gold and orange highlights of her skin were more prominent today. She wore a bronze and magenta shade of lipstick that made her lips the focal point of her face. She looked healthier. She was breath taking to say the least. Although she was still angry and distant, they were amicable. He was waiting on her to come around and understand why he had discussed her not returning to the facility with Jason. He needed to protect her. For whatever reason, he felt that she was his responsibility. More than anything, he loved living with her these last few days. He would have preferred that she not have been mad with him, but so be it. His eyes lingered too long on her face. That was why he almost missed the packed bags that surrounded her feet. "I thought we were going to the doctor. Have you been released, already?" He was puzzled as to what had changed.

Her eyes looked at everything, but him. "Uh, no you're right. We are going to the doctor, but I need to get out of this house. I'm getting a little claustrophobic. Besides, we both know that this isn't going to work. I don't like you making decisions for me without consulting me. Don't get me wrong, I am very grateful for your hospitality and for you taking care of me. I don't want to burden you any longer. I'm sure that I have stifled your social activities and interfered with your daily routine long enough." She knew that there must be a girlfriend somewhere with her "panties in a wad" because she had taken him out of commission for a few days.

Roxel knew that he was about to blow a gasket, the nerve of this woman to throw his hospitality back in his face. "Is there something mentally wrong with you or are you this difficult to get along with normally. I thought we had an understanding that I would take care of you until you were released by the doctor. And, I stand to be corrected, but that hasn't happened yet. So, if you're not released today, where do you plan to go?" He knew he was going to hate the answer before the words left his mouth. This woman was past irritating, she was a pain in the you-know-what. Maniacs were trying to kill her and she didn't have a clue. This whole scene was exhausting.

She could tell that he was madder than Hades. Oh God, this man was sinfully drop-dead gorgeous and her body was responding to him in a bad way. His left eye had a slight tic, his nose flared and his jaw was set in a scowl. That was just too bad. "I asked John if I could stay at his place if the doctor doesn't discharge me, today".

That did it. He had no self-control left. He had totally gone over the edge. He was absolutely speechless and if he opened his mouth, there were no nice words waiting to escape from it. She was unbelievable. "Pharise, you amaze me more and more."

She didn't quite know what to make out of that statement. But if looks could kill, she would be DOA. One thing she knew, she had better keep her mouth closed. He slowly ascended the stairs like some threatening animal, never allowing his eyes to falter from her eyes. If she had good sense, then she would have run. But, she didn't.

He had good home training and had never hit a woman before. However, this woman had invaded his senses and was wreaking havoc on his sanity. He was certain that they would eventually kill each other. Roxel had no idea what he would do or say to her when he reached the top stair. He was past angry and irate and was bordering on being livid. His chest tightened with each step he took which caused every breath to be painful. He stood toe-to-toe with her and her gaze didn't falter. She wasn't scared of him, but she should be.

She watched him, his eyes had darkened in anger and his flaring nostrils took on a life of their own. She would have fallen over her luggage, if he hadn't been holding her hands above her head as he forced her to step back into the wall. He pinned her to the wall with one hand securing her wrists and the other hand was on her back side pressing her to his groin. He was ranting about something, but for the life of her she couldn't understand a word he was saying. He felt so good. He fastened his lips to hers and he controlled the kiss. This wasn't a nice kiss, but an all consuming one. The words "no or stop" never entered her brain, which obviously diminished in size the moment he touched her. His tongue sought entry into her mouth and he latched on to her tongue sucking the very life out of her. She was levitating. He had lifted her off of the floor. His legs controlled her lower body stretching her to give him total access to her private area. His hands searched for her zipper and his hand cupped her mound and he continued to grind into her soft supple body. She was hot, burning up was more like it and that was making him hotter. He pushed the capris pants down her thick curvy legs.

She was mad at him and he was mad at her, but he was making her feel oh so good. She heard moans and groans that erupted from her mouth. Her panties dampened and she knew that he was quite aware of it, too. She couldn't believe that her body was betraying her. His touch set her on fire. His kisses had her hovering between reality and ecstasy. He used two fingers to taunt her and quickly inserted a finger to bring her to a climax. She wiggled to gain a better position. He rubbed her sensitive spot with the greatest amount of concentration. She leaned her head back into the wall giving him access to her thin neck. He sucked on it like a starving man. She didn't want to have anything to do with him, but he would give her something to remember this encounter. He sucked and nipped her neck, marking her. His head lowered to the hollow of her neck enjoying her sweetness. His tongue continued to explore her neck and moved lower to her breast. He lifted the white silky top to gather around her shoulders and sucked her nipples through her bra. He felt her soft flesh surrounding his fingers began to contract. Her breathing was loud and labored. She wasn't that unaffected by him as she put on. He would give anything to be inside her and pumping his seed into her warmth. *Where did that thought come from because he had never before in life given any woman his seed.* He heard her scream and her body went into spasms. He wouldn't allow his fingers to let up and continued to work her through three orgasms.

When he knew she was completely spent and couldn't take anymore, he raised her higher off the floor securing her legs over his shoulder. He pushed the thin red panties to the side and he devoured her. He licked all of her syrupy juices off and allowed his tongue to penetrate her core pushing it in as far as he could. His face was smashed to the apex of her legs that contained what he needed. Her body began to convulse again uncontrollably and she would have fallen if he had not tightened his hold around her waist. Her flaccid body slumped over his head. He gave her a few minutes to recover as he lowered her to the floor. He felt her stirring. He helped her up and assisted straightening her clothes.

"Now, I will meet you in the truck," he said with his anger returning. He picked up her luggage, turned, and walked down the stairs without saying another word.

Roxel Stapleton could teach classes on being a selfless passionate lover. Yea, he had jacked her up alright in the most sensual way. Her body was still humming and already missing his touch. His ministrations had sent her way over the edge. Her body had been dormant for five years. That was when she left Spencer Maxwell, her boyfriend of three of the most unfulfilling years of her life. He was a good looking pediatric surgeon with a Type "A" personality who believed that it was in her best interest that he dictate the direction her life should go. She had long since tired of their constant bickering. He had never asked how she felt about things or asked for her input. It was always about him. She realized that she was simply "arm candy" for him, a man ten years her senior. She couldn't remember him ever apologizing for all the cruel mean things he had done and said over the span of their relationship. He would give her wonderful gifts in hopes of atoning himself periodically. She was sure he loved her in some demented sort of way, but he probably had never been in love with her and her him. He was too busy being in love with himself. She rushed to the bathroom to clean up and half-ran out to the truck. It would take about twenty minutes to get to the appointment and they would be late if they didn't hurry. *Her life was getting more complicated by the day.*

Roxel knew that his actions bordered on insane. He was a man obsessed with a woman who wasn't giving him the time of day. She believed that he was an egotistical conceited alpha male who was consumed with his own agenda. She couldn't be farther off the mark. What she didn't know and he wouldn't bother divulging was that he was the man who was destined to make her his woman. He would not accept the minute pieces of herself that she parceled out to others. Anger had him seeing red. Their passion created a shift in the atmosphere. Once, he had gotten started there was no way he could stop. Her taste was "crack" addictive and he was unable to get enough. Initially, she probably wanted to rebuff his advances. He had taken control of the situation. He intended to seduce her into submitting to the truth. The truth was that there was an emotional connection between them. She might not verbalize it, but her body had confirmed the truth. She could go on and do whatever it was that she needed to do. Hopefully, she would realize that sometimes, people needed help from unlikely sources.

They rode to the appointment in silence. He drove faster than usual to get them there on time. His gaze never faltered from the road before him. Earlier, his eyes had registered anger, then passion and fire, and now again anger. They would get through the appointment without incident. Maybe, sometime in the future, they could return to being civil. However, he doubted that would be today.

Chapter 13

THEY BOTH ARRIVED at the doctor's office in one piece. The doctor entered her office. They had been placed in there about ten minutes ago. "I have some good news, Pharise and some bad news. Which would you rather hear, first? Carolyn liked Pharise and they seemed to connect instantaneously. Carolyn wondered about the hunk who had accompanied her to the doctor today. It would be interesting to see how things would play out between the two. Pharise eyed Roxel as a look of fear clouded her eyes. "We'll take the bad news first," he said.

"Pharise's shoulder is still swollen and it looks like the sprain is healing slowly. I would suggest a sling if I believed she would wear it, but I don't." "Pharise's lab was fine except that her white blood count is still elevated some. This leads me to believe she still has an infection, which I plan to aggressively treat with a stronger antibiotic. She is slightly anemic and this could be a result of her losing a considerable amount of blood when she was injured. I have prescribed some medicine for that. However, if her blood count drops lower, we will need to consider giving her a blood transfusion again. As a result Pharise, you won't be able to drive for at least another couple of weeks. I am concerned about her headaches and I am not totally convinced that they are stress headaches. I realize that it has been your preference not to take anything for them, but I believe that they are, at a minimum, a contributor to your insomnia. I hope you will consider taking this mild medication for the migraines to see if this gives you any relief.

She would not be released today. If fact, she would have under someone's care for the next few days. She had gotten better, but was still having symptoms associated with the concussion. Roxel did not know how things would work out between him and Pharise. He had spoken to his father earlier. Everything seemed to be quiet at the plant. They had scheduled several town hall meetings for the employees to keep them up to date on the safety issues that would be addressed in the coming months. Most of them were based on Pharise's assessment. Jessie and his team were getting closer to finding the people responsible for the accidents. Unbeknown to the employees, the hidden security cameras were capturing a lot of valuable information that were pieces to the puzzle. Jessie had also mentioned Pharise's photos that provided still images of some of the employees tampering with equipment. The union president and some stewards had contacted him to get a meeting set up to reinstitute some of the overtime. His father said he thought that was unusual, since he had been hearing over the years that the employees complained about not having time to spend with their families. "There was something rotten in the state of Denmark". His father expressed that it was good to be back at the helm for a few days even though it would be short lived. Dad loved his retirement and loved spending time with his wife. That was one of the things which brought him regret when he was building the company.

He, his father, and other board members had been interviewing for the position of facility manager for about two months and had a short list of three people. It was time for him to move on from this interim position and get his focus back to running the company.

The family dinner together was scheduled in the next couple of days. His father had suggested that he bring Pharise. He had confided in his dad the challenges they were having. They certainly had a lot of bumps in the road. "Usually, I wouldn't even spend this much time considering an issue like this. If I was in a relationship and either of us wanted to dissolve it, that's what we did. This whole relationship thing on this level is foreign to me and I seem to be botching it up on a regular basis."

His dad had simply laughed at him, saying a woman is not like a business and that I couldn't use the same tactics on her that I used at work.

"Pharise, I want you to understand that it is difficult to heal physically when you are not healing mentally. You will need to take your medicine. Pharise blew out a slow breath. "Ok, I'll try it your way. It's obvious that my way isn't working. Can I go back to my hotel room? I feel like I'm up to staying by myself."

The doctor tapped an ink pen unconsciously on the desk. "I know you wish that my answer was yes, but unfortunately I'm going to have to say no. Your symptoms still worry me along with the infection and low blood count. I would hate for something to happen and you have no family or friends checking on you".

Although the doctor's visit had lightened her mood and she was really enjoying Roxel's company, she felt it best that she continue with her plans to stay with John for a few days. "I'll comply with your suggestions". Her next appointment was in one week. If things looked better she would be discharged at this time.

"There's one more thing. You need a need a bag of IV fluids to combat a little electrolyte imbalance from the blood loss. You can stop by the emergency room or I can get a home health nurse to come to where you're staying. What area of the city are you living?"

She could tell Roxel was staring at her profile waiting to hear what she would say. After this morning's encounter, she wasn't sure she trusted herself around Roxel. He was all consuming and she didn't know how to tell him, no. In fact, when he was touching her and kissing her, she lost all inhibitions as she allowed him to take her to a place of pure passion. This was a place she had never been before and she was terrified of that. She gave the doctor John's address. They both heard Roxel forcibly blowing air from his mouth at her statement.

"I actually live around the corner from that address. Will the person you're staying with mind you getting the IV in their home?"

"No, he won't mind." For some reason, she felt really bad. Roxel had gone out of his way to accommodate her and to make things comfortable and it seemed she was throwing his hospitality back in his face, but she wasn't. What Roxel didn't know was that being in such close quarters with him was a little unnerving. His presence literally turned her on. His smile sent her to another orbit. Literally she could still feel his mouth pressed to the base of her neck.

She made a few calls. "I can stop by after I leave work, which will be about five-thirty. I should be there around six fifteen at the latest. I can hang the bag of IV and that way we can chat a little more."

Pharise lips turned up into a huge smile. "That would be great." She would enjoy talking some more with the doctor. She was in desperate need of a female friend.

She and Roxel walked out of the doctor's office and she wondered if the doctor spent that much time with all of her patients. She was grateful that she had taken time with her. Roxel's shoulder lacked the rigidness that he usually exhibited and his face was masked. She knew that she was the cause of it. She didn't want a confrontation out in public, so she would wait until they got in the car to try and explain. She hoped that he would have an open mind. She had a feeling that things wouldn't go as smoothly as she desired.

Chapter 14

ROXEL AND PHARISE left the doctor's office together and rode in silence towards John's home for what seemed like eternity. She couldn't tell what he was thinking. She folded and unfolded her hands in her lap like a juvenile. He finally glanced in her direction. "So, what is it Pharise? Did I offend you or am I simply not your type? I'm a big boy and I prefer if you were honest with me." He didn't really know if he wanted to hear what she had to say. Experience revealed that she was brutally honest. And the heaviness he felt squeezing his chest was almost unbearable. He realized earlier that day that Pharise was a dangerous woman and she held all the cards. She was dangerous to his sanity and his emotions. When it came to her, he had no control of his responses to her. Not only was this unfamiliar territory, this territory was more like a mine field. He simply didn't know the next step to take. His mind told him to walk away, but his heart said otherwise.

She stared at her hands. She knew she was too much of a coward to face him. "Roxel, it's not personal. I would prefer to be by myself. I need to spend some time to figure out what I'm going to do for the next thirty years. Initially, I was angry with you and Jason for shutting me out of the investigation and I accused you both of trying to control my life. I don't think that is the real reason that I am wary of getting too close to you. I have too many demons to deal with and too much baggage that I'm carrying around. You heard the doctor. I am a work in progress and it's not likely that I am going to get myself together in the next few days or maybe not even in a year. That wouldn't be fair to get involved in any kind of relationship. We come from a different kind of people and we travel in totally different circles. There's no way I would fit nicely into your life. I know you believe that I am involved with John, but I'm not. He's a friend.

That's it. I've had bad relationships in my past and I don't know if I am willing to take another chance. Sometimes, when we're together everything seems so good and other times I feel like my life is falling apart. I appreciate your kindness and thank you for showing me one of the best times in my life. Please don't hate me. I really do like you more than you'll ever know, but I don't think that I'm the right girl for you." She wondered if she made any sense at all and whether he could understand any of the things she had said. What she couldn't tell him was that where he was concerned, she knew that things were way over her head.

Oddly enough, Roxel understood what Pharise had said. Only God knew how he could. They were both "works in progress", she for one reason and he another. She hadn't told the truth when she said that this wasn't personal. This was as personal as it got. He knew that pushing her into something that she wasn't ready for would be disastrous. So, he would wait until she came to him of her own free will. He wouldn't wait long, but he would wait. And he wouldn't stand by idly and wait, he would help her along. He remembered what his father had said about Pharise not being able to be handled like business deal. His parents raised him to never back down from a challenge and this definitely was a challenge. Without her realizing it, he would turn the tables on Pharise. He would allow her to become the hunter and he would become the prey. By the time she realized what was happening, she would be too far gone. "Pharise, I want you to know something. This thing between us is not over by a long shot. I'm going to give you some space because you're asking for it. However, I will not allow you to turn your back on what is developing between us. And, I absolutely detest the fact that you are leaving my home and going to John's home. I will respect that this is your decision, but I want you to know that I do not like it. You can't run away from your problems and it is my intention to help you deal with whatever is causing you all this pain. I can only do that if you allow me. So, it looks like the ball is in your court and the next move is yours."

It seemed that they had come to an impasse, although they understood each other's position better. Pharise was lost in her thoughts as she leaned her head back on the soft leather of his Lexus. It was a breezy afternoon and she hadn't thought to pack a sweater. She turned on the heat controlled seat and allowed the mellow sounds of James Ingram coming through the radio to relax her. She hadn't realized that she had fallen asleep until she heard Roxel's promptings for her to wake up. Her eyes slowly fluttered open and she turned her head to catch a sneak glimpse of the incredibly attractive man who stirred her inner being. She hadn't realized that he was also watching her. Their gazes held for a few moments and the spell was broken when he said, "we're here at John's." She gathered her purse and waited for him to round the car to open her door. He extended his hand to help her exit the car and she immediately felt a rush of unnatural heat coursing in her veins. She knew he felt it also because his eyes communicated that he refused to act like their attraction did not exist. He allowed her hand to go and retrieved the luggage from the trunk. Their steps were in perfect union as they walked the path to John's home. He pushed the door bell and waited. She tried to divert her gaze so she wouldn't have to deal with the good-bye. He refused to let that happen. He tilted her chin upward with his finger and she saw him lower his mouth to hers. This kiss wasn't a controlling one. This kiss communicated that he understood her inner turbulence. It was a drugging kiss that she wished would never stop. He took his tongue and rimmed her lips and then nibbled at the corners of her mouth. This was the way they were when John answered the door.

Chapter 15

ROXEL HAD REFUSED to come inside. He handed John her luggage. His lips grazed hers and he turned and headed for his car. He never looked back. She watched that sexy swagger until he opened his car door and drove off. His leaving seemed to leave a big hole in her heart. She would survive. She had been surviving all of her life.

John's home was exquisite. His home reminded her of the houses she had seen in New Mexico with the rounded roofs. The colors inside, also, reminded her of the Mexican homes she had seen with the robust colors. "I love it. Did you do all of this?"

"Yea, I lived in New Mexico for about seven years. I loved the "old town" feel and look. I attempted to recreate that same essence here. Mi casa es tu casa." John showed her around and she loved everything she saw. He showed her to the room she would be using for the next few days.

She had died and gone to heaven. Her smile was huge as she eyed the colorful Mexican quilt on the bed with Mexican tapestry on the walls. The bathroom was like a spa with a large Jacuzzi and an open shower. She and John talked for the next couple of hours after she unpacked her clothes and placed them in a drawer. He had prepared a light meal. They watched some old movies in between and talked some about the incidents at the facility.

John felt that he needed to have his say about her and Roxel. "You know that you're running from Roxel. How long do you plan on doing that? He's doesn't appear to be the type of man that will be put off for long. I suggest you figure out what you're going to do about your relationship with him."

"We don't have a relationship, John. I don't even know if I would go so far as to say that we are even friends. Sometimes we really get each other and other times we're at each other's throats."

"That kiss certainly didn't look like "nothing" and the marks covering your neck certainly don't look like nothing".

"Oh, well that was just a good-bye kiss", she was saying this as she left the room in search of a mirror. She remembered Roxel kissing her neck, but she didn't remember seeing any marks on her neck. She had dressed in a hurry and only looked in the mirror to comb her hair and touch up her make-up. She didn't have to look hard to see the red and purple splotches lining her neck. As she opened her blouse, he had also marked her breast and stomach. Just remembering him placing them there caused heat to rush to her core and then she felt a gush of moisture in her panties. Roxel Stapleton, indeed, made her hot down to her bones. No man had ever made her feel this good and now she was aroused. That's what she was trying to tell him, he did things to her that kept her off kilter and she didn't know if she liked that.

Pharise returned to the great room and tried without success to avoid John's face with the biggest grin on it. There was no way she could down play the marks visibly covering her neck. "Whatever, John", she drawled in her best Southern accent and John laughed a hearty laugh. There was no use trying to explain what happened this morning was a one-time incident. She had a feeling Roxel had no intention of it being that. He was an unselfish lover. When she last counted she had four or five orgasms that nearly blew the roof off her head, but she hadn't had the chance to return the favor. He didn't seem 'put off' about that in the least. "I really like him, but I don't know if it will go anywhere".

John nodded understanding my meaning. Their conversation was interrupted by a ringing doorbell. John probably had company coming. She would retreat to her room and give him his space when she saw Carolyn following him back into the room.

"Oh, I forgot John that she has to give me an IV. My memory hasn't been too good lately." She could tell that John wasn't upset about the intrusion at all. It was obvious he couldn't take his eyes off the fine doctor. Pharise introduced the two and briefly told John about today's visit with her and her recommendations.

Dr. Trapson entered and instantly changed the atmosphere of the room. She was a breath of fresh air. "Is there somewhere I can set this IV pole up? It would be fine if you set it up by the lounger where you could lean back and relax. If you have a TV table, I could use it to put my things on and start her IV."

John retrieved a small breakfast table from the kitchen. She brought everything she needed to create a sterile environment. Pharise relaxed in the lounger and turned her head away from the doctor as she started the IV.

John was watching her closely. John asked, "Do you need anything else?"

"It would be great if you have some water or a sprite and some crackers. Sometimes, the IV makes people sick to their stomachs."

John went back to the kitchen and brought back two tables filled with light foods and beverages. It would take about an hour-and-a-half for the IV to go in.

"Have you eaten?" John asked Carolyn.

This question should have been a bit forward under normal circumstances, but it didn't feel that way at all with the doctor. "Actually, I haven't had a chance to eat anything since breakfast. I had errands to run during lunch. Why, do I look like I need to eat?" Carolyn was laughing at John's embarrassment. Carolyn took a seat near Pharise, grabbed a sandwich and she begin talking like they had been friends for years.

John grabbed a sandwich from Carolyn's tray and he noticed that didn't seem to bother the gorgeous doctor. Her thick spiral natural curls danced around her face. Her golden eyes were vibrant and shined with mischief. He could tell she liked having fun. He bobbed his head to look at her finger to see if she was wearing a wedding ring. There was no evidence of one. He relaxed and continue to stare at the beautiful doctor. They were all laughing and telling stories for the next two hours. Both helped Carolyn pack up. The IV made Pharise a little tired. She bid them both a good night. She planned to hook up with Carolyn on Saturday to get some shopping in and to hang out. She left to go to her room, shower, and get into bed.

John helped Carolyn with her bag and followed her to her roomy Suburban SUV. He liked the view from behind and he walked slowly to make sure he didn't miss anything. He had never appreciated nice full hips until now. His mouth watered. She had to have known that he was watching her. Obviously, it didn't bother her. Her body moved with the easiness of the waves of the ocean. He placed her things in the truck. After assisting getting her in the truck, he stood at the door. She turned her body to face him. "I am glad that Pharise needed that IV". They both laughed. She had the prettiest smile. He decided to take a chance. "Are you available tomorrow to come by? I'm having a cook-out and you would be my date." He wanted her to be clear on the fact that he wanted to date her. Prior to this conversation, he hadn't planned on having a cook-out, but he would quickly remedy that if she agreed. He hoped she was considering agreeing.

She really liked the brooding attorney. He was a hunk in every sense of the word. He looked a little older than the men she normally dated. Good old fashioned fun was a rarity these days. John had a wicked sense of humor. She had never dated European men, but she was fiercely attracted to him. "Yea, I would like that."

"Is 6:30 good for you or is later better", John asked.

"That's perfect. I live about fifteen minutes away from here. It will give me ample time to go home and change. I've been dying for some good food. I'm usually too tired to cook when I get home and I'll pop in a Lean Cuisine. Do I need to bring anything?"

"Yes, bring a swim suit and that smile". Her reaction to that was just what he hoped. Her luscious full lips turned up into a huge smile.

"I can do that".

He leaned in across her and buckled her seatbelt. His lips brushed across hers. He told her to drive safely and closed her door.

He watched her until her vehicle turned the corner and he walked back inside. He prayed that his luck with women had changed for the better. He closed and locked his door and couldn't wait for tomorrow's cook-out. He needed to invite one other person and plan his menu.

He picked up the phone to call his friend who was probably quite perturbed with him because Pharise had decided to stay at his home. Roxel picked up on the second ring. "Is anything wrong with her?" John heard the concern and hurt in his voice. "No, she's fine. The doctor came by and gave her the IV. She mentioned she was tired and went to bed a little while ago. I was calling to invite you to a cook-out tomorrow. Are you available? I invited the doctor over and thought you might round things out."

"Are you match-making or trying to pick a fight?"

"Neither, I don't think you or Pharise need any help from me. That kiss on my porch was anything but platonic. It was enough to start a small inferno. And, she hadn't even noticed all the marks on her neck and God knows where until I brought it to her attention. *John laughed.* I just thought you might want to come. If it's a problem, I have a couple of other guys who I can call. I'm sure they wouldn't have a problem entertaining and keeping her company." Roxel let out so many expletives that John had to take the phone away from my ear to keep the heat from coming through.

Roxel said, "Yea, I'll be there. What do I need to bring? Does she know that I am coming?"

"You can bring anything you like to put on the grill and bring your swim trunks. And, no she doesn't know."

"Ok and, thanks for the invite. I owe you." Roxel disconnected the telephone. It was obvious that the good doctor had made quite an impression on John for him to be planning a cook-out. Pharise had filled his thoughts for the last few hours. He had gotten some paper work done and was now relaxing on his sofa with a glass of wine. He really needed something stiffer, but he had sworn off strong alcohol a couple of years ago. It seemed she always pushed him to the limit. The rational thing to have done was to have dragged her kicking and screaming back to his home. He hadn't and that was surprising in itself. He thought about calling her since the moment he left her at John's door, but had decided against it. Sanity lost out when he picked up the telephone and dialed her number.

"Hello," came the sweetest voice he had ever heard.

"I was checking to see how you were doing and how the IV had gone."

"It went fine. I think John likes Carolyn and vice versa. They couldn't take their eyes off of each other. They were hilarious. I'm mad at you. You left all of those marks all over my neck and other places." She smiled.

"Are you mad at me for placing them there or are you mad that they were visible?" He knew he was goading her.

She thought about the question and answered truthfully. I'm mad because they were visible. It allows people to make assumptions about our relationship."

"Well, next time I might consider being a little more discreet. I can't control what other people think. I'm only concerned about what you think. If you were here, you would be in my bed."

"You are so arrogant, you know. How are you able to carry around that big head of yours," she chuckled.

"No, I just know what I want and I will do everything in my power to have what I want. My parents raised us to go after what we wanted in life and to never back down from a challenge."

Pharise asked, "Are we talking about your life's ambitions or me?"

"Both. Get some sleep. Tonight, dream about something that is pleasant. If you have a bad night, give me a call so that I can help you through it. "Good night".

"Good night", Pharise whispered.

John solicited Pharise's help in preparing for an off-the-chain cook-out. He mentioned that he invited Carolyn. He had lots of food. She marinated some ribs, chops, chicken, and steaks earlier that day while he was at work. Southerners were known to put everything on the grill. John was busy preparing fruit salads, salsa, vegetables and sorbet. He was an exceptional cook. He used fresh vegetables and spices. Pharise preferred charcoal grills to gas and was glad that he shared her sentiments. Pharise wanted to shower before his guest came, but she felt comfortable with some short shorts on and with an oversized t-shirt. The meat was smoking nicely. John made her some fruity non-alcoholic frozen drink that was simply delicious. At six everything was ready and Pharise put all the meat in the double oven to keep it warm. She was walking to her room to shower and change when the doorbell rang. John shouted for her to get the door. Pharise looked through the peep hole and Roxel appeared larger than life. She was sick of everyone keeping her in the dark. Did everyone think that she needed help running her life? She was acting crazy. She knew she wanted to see him. She re-grouped and opened the door. A slow easy smile covered her face when she saw him juggling slaw, kabobs of shrimp, and a huge pitcher of another fruity drink. Pharise took the slaw out of his hands and headed toward the kitchen. She turned her head to look in his face, "good to see you". A smirk crossed his face when he said, "I like the shorts".

"Yea, I bet you do. Why didn't you tell me last night that you were coming over for the barbecue? No one seems to tell me anything."

"Am I in trouble for not telling you?" Roxel chuckled.

"No". The smile was lit up her face.

"Good. I am expecting a proper greeting. Are you still running scared" Roxel asked?

They met up with John in the kitchen. "Hey John. Thanks for the invitation. Do you have an open spot on the grill for the shrimp?"

"Yea, it's all clear." Pharise had taken all the other meat off. John was finishing up everything. Pharise led him out back to the patio. He loaded the grill with the shrimp. Roxel grabbed Pharise's hand before she scurried away and pulled her close to his length.

"Roxel, I smell like smoke and I need to take a shower and change into something more appropriate." He nibbled on the side of her neck and inched up to her sweet lips. She leaned into him and he captured her lips. He pressed her body closer to him and his hand as he caressed her back side. He was slowly grinding her and she was enjoying it immensely. He thrust his tongue into her mouth simulating the thrusting from making love and she came right there. An orgasm hit her without warning weakening her knees and causing her to lose control of her limbs. Roxel held onto her tightly. Otherwise, she would have fallen. When it had passed, he merely smiled. "I am glad to see you. Are you glad I came?"

He hadn't "come" at all. She had been the one to come outside standing up. She wondered how he was able to do that. He must have had an awful lot of practice. "Roxel, I plan to get you back in spades." He looked taken aback at her forwardness. That's exactly what she wanted. She wanted to shake him up a little. "I am going to shower and change clothes, alone. Watch your shrimp." She turned and headed back in the house. He poured him a cup of Sangria and worked the grill anticipating her return.

Carolyn had arrived as she was heading to change. "I'll see you in a minute after I shower," she yelled. She showered and imagined Roxel sharing the shower with her. If Roxel wanted a little seduction, she would give it to him. Earlier she planned to wear some walking shorts, but she changed her mind. She pulled out some cut off jean shorts and paired it with a clingy peach top that ended at her belly button. She pulled out a peach shirt that she could use as a cover if it cooled off outside. She pulled her hair up and twisted it on top of her head with runaway curls landing around her face. She added some lip gloss, eyeliner, and bronze eye shadow. Her facial scars were healing nicely. She had been using vitamin E oil to minimize the scarring. She walked out toward the kitchen. John and the others had taken all the food outdoors. She opened the patio door and stepped out. She was hungry and couldn't wait to eat. John said, "We were waiting on you to eat". She greeted Carolyn who had pulled her hair into a pony tail, which hung down her back. She was a natural beauty. She had added some bronze highlights to her face to make her appear more striking. She was wearing lime walking shorts and a fitted lime top with a coverlet.

Roxel asked Pharise what she wanted to eat. He offered to fix her plate. "Give me a little of everything. I'll go back if I want more of something." She sat in one of the loungers and relaxed with good friends, good food and good conversation. They had all eaten way too much. They all headed for the pool next. John had a pool-side dressing room. The guys finished changing first and were already in the pool. Carolyn sashayed down to the pool almost causing John's eyes to pop out of his head. Each couple swam and played together retreating into separate worlds. John and Roxel swam several laps. John and Carolyn got out and went inside for a while to watch a movie. Roxel continued swimming laps. He finally swam to her.

"Are you afraid of going out to far?" Roxel asked.

"I'm not a good swimmer. I've always been afraid to go out in the deep water".

Her hesitancy and fear was written all over her face. If she wanted to get beyond some of these issues, she would have to face her fears. He wasn't a psychiatrist by any means. One thing he knew about and that was facing ones fears tended to help you manage them better. "Do you trust me Pharise?"

She trusted him, but she didn't trust going out there in that deep water. She could tell he was waiting on an answer. He was so irritating sometimes.

"Yes, I trust you". This was said with a degree of hesitation. Her confidence in people tended to waver given the various circumstances. This vacation was about moving ahead with her life and ridding herself of those things that placed barriers in her way. She extended her hand to Roxel and he accepted it. Roxel taught her to float on her back, tread water, and swim under water in a short amount of time. She wouldn't go so far as to say she was a natural, but she had a lot of fun playing in the water. They both laughed at her blunders and splashed water like they were toddlers.

She noticed that Roxel hadn't attempted to kiss her since coming to the house after their initial greeting. He was considerate and caring, but he hadn't touched or caressed her like she wanted. Roxel had been clear when he told her that the ball was in her court. He would wait on her to make the next move if she chose to do so. A life filled with boundaries was a life where a person simply existed rather than lived. Today, she wanted to live. *She would "take no thought of tomorrow".*

"Where did you go when you just zoned out?" Roxel asked.

"I was just thinking of how much I missed you and I was just wondering about us".

His eyes bore into my soul. Somehow, they were able to communicate with each other without saying a word. Pharise had his undivided attention and he was truly listening to her. His body partially submerged in the water as they talked and she continued to play in the water. Without warning her body yearned to be close to him, to touch him. She didn't allow her inner voice to talk her out of it. She realized she was standing directly in front of him when Pharise stopped moving. Her hand traced his sensual mouth and those mystical eyes that seem to hold me hostage with their gaze. She had the overwhelming desire to taste his lips. Pharise took no thought of John and Carolyn or where we were. Her lips came down on him with a hunger that was foreign. It was as if she was famished and only he could satisfy her. He lifted her to straddle his body, facing him. The fire continued to build inside of her as she felt his large hands roaming over her body. He pinched her nipples and massaged her breast through the yellow two-piece she had purchased the other day when Carolyn and she went shopping. Both the women had both thought it was a hot swim suit. The thin strips of material barely covered her breasts or hips, but Pharise thought it would be quite tempting. Roxel had turned the tables. She was the one being tempted. She knew that she should stop. She could hear his heart beat. Pharise prayed for common sense to kick in. She wanted to taste him, all of him. Her mouth latched onto the taut skin under his ear. She nibbled, sucked, and nipped the sweet and salty flesh. Pharise sucked harder to guarantee that he would remember this coming together. He pushed the bikini bottom over to the side as he allowed his fingers to chart a sensual course. The sweet sounds she made took his breath away. She reached inside his trunks massaging his throbbing prodigiousness. She hadn't realized he had sheathed himself. And then, she nodded her head in agreement of his next move. He entered her in one swift movement allowing the buoyancy of the water to further ignite their passion. John and Carolyn were inside watching a movie they assumed. Even if they had not been, neither would have been able to stop the most delicious lovemaking either had ever experienced. And then, it happened. He felt the tightening in his scrotum and couldn't take another breath. Pharise's head leaned back and he teased her breast when she begin to groin out her passion as one orgasm after another overtook her. His world stood still and then tilted as he released his passion inside of barrier. He held her as their breathing returned to normal. They were both drawn out of this sensual haze when they heard voices coming closer. Pharise straightened her swim suit quickly and attempted to move off his lap. He was having none of that as he held her firmly in place. "Roxel let me up. I don't want them to see us looking like we were making out in the pool." She looked a little frantic and put out.

"Let me get this straight." His eyes had lost their warmth. "We were all over each other a minute ago when no one was around. Now, you don't want them to see us being affectionate. Why do you care what someone else thinks about us being together? I don't know what they've been doing since they left. That's none of my business." He was angry with her, again. She had just ruined one of the most intimate moments that he ever shared with a woman. Obviously, she had problems with her sexuality or either she was playing games. He didn't know if he would be around long enough to find out the answer to either of these questions. He removed his hand from her thighs as John and Carolyn came into view. Reluctantly, he assisted her to her feet. He was still fuming. He hoped that it was not noticeable, but that was probably unlikely.

Carolyn came to the edge of the pool as Pharise walked up to meet her. "I came to say good night". She glanced my way with a smile as big as Texas. Obviously, the two had enjoyed each other's company. "I have hospital rounds early in the morning." She told Pharise that she would see her on Saturday. John was holding her hand as he escorted her to her car. They really looked like they were into each other.

"I think I better be leaving, also, Pharise. Have a good night." He felt that it was time for him to leave. He was turning to leave.

"Why are you leaving so soon? I was hoping to talk some more." Pharise asked.

Roxel wasn't sure what was going on with her or why she was so conflicted. She had to figure out what she really wanted. He couldn't help her with that.

"Come home with me", he said. His eyes were glazed with passion and anger.

He could read her like a book. She was hot one minute and cold the next. He knew before she said it what her answer would be. He didn't want to hear the word, 'no'. Before she could answer, he turned again to leave. "You have a good night."

She stood in the same spot immobilized by her own screwed up issues. Would she ever be able to move forward? If she continued to push people away, she would end up alone". It was up to her to figure out what she needed to do to keep from losing him. The first thing that she needed to focus on was her fears. Then she would figure out what she needed to do to get back in Roxel's good grace.

Roxel was intercepted by John on his way out. "What's the rush?"

"John now is not the time to give me your nickel and dime speech. It is obvious that Pharise and I are going nowhere fast. She sends out mixed messages and I am way too old and too tired to try and figure it all out. She refuses to accept my hospitality. Yet, she can stay here with you. I'm tired of trying."

"No you're not. Frustration is ruling you. Give her a little time. It's obvious that she's afraid to let you get too close. That hasn't stopped you from cornering a place in her heart. She just needs to get her head and heart on one accord in order to give this thing you have a chance. Don't give up on her."

Roxel heard what he was saying, but his heart hurt. He couldn't get through to her. "We'll see. Good night". He made it to his car and then he was gone.

John entered the house and secured the alarm. Pharise was sitting in the entertainment room in the dark. It was clear that she been crying. "You want to talk about it?"

"No, but thanks anyway." She kissed John on the cheek and headed for her bedroom. Tomorrow would be better. She was devastated that she had messed up, again. Soon, she thought, she would make it right. She showered and readied for bed. If sanity ruled, she would pick up the telephone and call him. She'd explain why she preferred not staying with him. She was still an old fashion girl and didn't believe in sharing a home with a man unless they were married. She believed that staying with a man was the reason her last relationship hadn't worked. Spencer and she had lived together two years. Their relationship was an emotional disaster for her. Spencer probably felt different about that. In fact, he verbalized that he had seen nothing wrong with their relationship. Living together allowed her to become a novelty to him. She was convenient and he felt there was no need to work on their relationship. He simply did what he wanted, but expected her to act like the obedient little wife. She had no intention of playing that role ever again. It was at that point in their relationship that things began to deteriorate quickly. Arguments followed. She then saw him for the selfish controlling idiot that he was. He would even try to order for her when they went to a restaurant without even asking what she wanted. She had tired of this and the other emotional abuse that was prominent in their union. It was then that she made preparation to find her own place and leave him and all that they had shared together. One day she packed a few odds and ends and a few clothes and left the luxurious home that she helped create. She never looked back and she never regretted leaving. Spencer had tried calling her numerous times, but she never returned any of his calls. He even tried coming to the hospital to talk to her, but she had informed the other staff members that they had broken up and she didn't want to see him. He soon got the message and moved on with his life. She had received an invitation to his wedding around the same time her mother had passed. She sent him and his new bride, a fellow surgeon, a gift and wished them well. She was truly happy for them.

Chapter 16

OXEL LOST HIMSELF in work. He had gone back to the plant. They were making good headway in finding the men responsible for the accidents. Jessie had been working on some photos from the security camera. One of the men in the dark sedan that followed Pharise was a known felon and a "whatever" man. That meant he would do whatever someone paid him to do. They suspected that the union was involved somehow and were working that angle. They also suspected someone in the front office with seeping information to these culprits. Everyone was keeping their eyes and ears open. They also limited the information that went out. Everything was scrutinized to a need to know basis.

They were also preparing for their annual board of director's benefit. It would be held on next Saturday. The board of directors and their families sponsored this event for large stock holders and the salaried staff members. Community leaders and politicians would also be in attendance. He hadn't spoken with Pharise in two weeks by his own choosing. The event was usually held in one of the local hotels. However, this year his parents had decided to host it at their home. Their home boasted of more than fifteen thousand square feet of living place. His mother loved entertaining and had talked his dad into including an entertainment gallery when the house was designed. This room was probably much larger and elegant than any hotel ballroom one could rent. This was his parents' way of giving something back to the board and employees who had worked so hard during the year. He was expected to be the toast master. He usually brought a date, but he had chosen to go solo this year. He had a couple of women on speed dial who would gladly accept an invitation to attend this function. He was certain that it would make the local papers and even some of the entertainment magazines. He was tired of pretentious relationships that were superficial at best. He would attend this one alone.

Pharise wondered what Roxel was doing. She knew he had returned to the facility from John and Jessie. Jessie had been keeping her up to date on the progress of the case. They had narrowed things down to about six suspects at the plant, but they weren't going to make a move until they could determine who the mastermind was behind all of this. The person was affiliated with the union in some way, but didn't have any particulars. They, also, suspected someone in a management position was feeding these criminals information. They didn't have any idea of the identity of this person. She still wasn't allowed to go there. She performed tasks for the case from her hotel room.

She enjoyed spending a few days with John. It had given her some human contact which she was beginning to need. They had visited several restaurants and gone to a few art museums when he came home from work. A couple of times Carolyn joined them. It seemed that they were getting to know each other. They never made her feel like a third wheel. Afterwards, they would return back to John's place and talk some more. During the day, she wandered through the city revisiting some of her favorite sites. It was a good day. The only thing missing was someone to share her experiences. She'd called Roxel again and his phone went straight to voice mail.

Today, she was having brunch at a local restaurant near the hotel. She had seen it yesterday on her return to the hotel. There were tables outside the establishment arranged like a Paris café. It was her intention to get some exercise in. She had been cooped up recuperating from the accident for more than two weeks. She had become a little claustrophobic and was dying to get out and get some fresh air.

The café was almost filled when she arrived. It looked like everyone had the same ideas as she did. The waitress appeared to be a young college student. Her animated personality would make for a pleasant morning. She preferred to have a table on the outside. They were weaving through the tables when Pharise heard her name being called. She turned toward the voices. Immediately, she saw Roxel's mother and sister waving from a nearby table. Pharise snaked her way toward them. *What were they doing her? She wondered.* "Good morning," she said with the biggest and brightest smile Pharise had seen in a long time. "It is a surprise seeing you here. This is one of my daughter's hang-outs. Tanya, this is Pharise Mallard, Roxel's friend." She could see the wheels turning in Mrs. Stapleton's eyes. She was definitely something else. "Tanya and I were putting some last minute touches on the benefit gala coming up."

She tried to hide that dumbfounded look that suddenly appeared on her face, but believed she failed miserably. She didn't know anything about a gala.

Mrs. Stapleton recognized the unspoken look in Pharise' face and went on to explain about the benefit as well as to invite Pharise. "Roxel must have forgotten to mention it to you," she said as a way of apologizing for his behavior. There was no way she could miss that look in Pharise's eyes that left as quickly as it came. It was a look that said I'm falling in love, but her hesitance indicated her relationship with Roxel might not be easy. It was, also, obvious that Roxel's mother knew he was probably not an easy man to love, but she was positive he would be worth the trouble. Roxel was handling this situation like he normally handled challenging ones that weren't related to business. He avoided them. It looked like he was avoiding Pharise, but she was rooting for Pharise.

Pharise thought of Mrs. Stapleton like a mother. She told her the truth. 'Roxel is a little put out with me right now. The truth is that I'm not even sure he's talking to me. I've tried calling him a few times, but it seems he's not taking my calls." She wouldn't tell his mother everything, but she didn't want her to think it was all Roxel's fault. "I didn't accept the hospitality that he extended to me appropriately. I haven't been in a serious relationship in about two years and to tell you the truth, Roxel's presence was a little suffocating to me. I've unintentionally pushed him away a couple of times. Unfortunately, I can now see the error of my ways and things don't look promising at all. I thought that I couldn't deal with my personal issues that were plaguing me with him around. I was wrong. I truly miss his company." She took a sip of the sparkling water she had ordered allowing it to remove the emotions lodged in her throat.

Mrs. Stapleton and Tanya were laughing. Apparently they were enjoying a joke that Pharise was not privy to. Tanya said, "Oh, don't you worry about messing up. We all do, especially when it comes to relationships. No one is perfect. Although, Roxel may think that he is. He thinks that he can handle everything like he would in the business. That is so far from the truth. I believe that you have made a monumental impact on my brother, which is a miracle. He doesn't let women get too close to him. He believes he doesn't have time for a committed relationship because he invests so much of himself in the business." His sister was all smiles.

"Yes, my husband has warned him not to become consumed in the business and forget about living and enjoying life. I think that somewhere along the way he has forgotten that advice. "Pharise, I am not into match making. I believe that my children are intelligent enough to make wise decisions about their mates on their own. If you and Roxel become an item, I would be forever grateful. I think that you would be a great asset to him and him to you. However, my son is quite stubborn. Obviously, you have crossed him. That is a hurdle you may need a little help crossing. Are you willing to receive some help?"

She looked into two loving smiling faces that had no hidden agenda other than to make sure Roxel was happy. "Yes, I'll accept a little help." Pharise didn't know if she was making the right decision, but she didn't want to be at odds with Roxel.

The meal was simply fabulous and the company was just as great. Mrs. Stapleton insisted that Pharise call her Tristan. There was no way that she could do that. Her mother would roll over in her grave. They talked about everything, but mostly girl talk. Tanya and I planned to go shopping after brunch so that I could find a gown for the gala. She had decided to go whether she was on speaking terms with Roxel or not. Two hours later, Mrs. Stapleton settled the bill, after they protested against her doing so. There was simply no talking her out of it. They had also invited her to dinner tonight. She didn't even ask if Roxel would be there. She wouldn't worry about that. She told herself that she was going as a friend of Mrs. Stapleton and Tanya. This wasn't the whole truth. Even if Roxel wasn't speaking to her, she still wanted to see him. He was the man who consumed her thoughts in the day and her dreams at night.

Pharise arrived promptly at five fifteen at the Stapleton's home that spanned about what seemed like two blocks in a secluded area. She pushed the button at the security gate and announced her name. The gate swung open and allowed her entry. She drove for another half mile before her rental stopped at a circular drive that was lined with four other luxury cars. There was a hot little red corvette that was simply adorable. Pharise wondered who the owner of that one was. She stood at the over-sized door pondering if she should ring the bell or return to her car and high tail it out of there. She was way out of her league. When she looked all around this spread, it was further validated. She lost her nerve at that moment.

Pharise's hand dropped back to her side and she was turning to leave when the door swung over and she was enveloped in a big sisterly hug from Tanya. Tanya was gorgeous in a pink linen suit and pink and blue shell. Her hair fell around her shoulders in large brown loose curls. Her hypnotic eyes and thin nose gave made her appear to look more like an islander. She wore very little make-up. She didn't have to wear any. She pulled me in and whispered, "you were about to lose your nerve, weren't you. Don't let all this stuff intimidate you. My family is as down to earth as they come. We have never allowed things to define us. So, don't go sabotaging your happiness before you can get in the door." She was smiling as the words rolled off her tongue. "Come on in. You can help us finish everything."

She liked that idea immensely. She followed Tanya as she gave a brief tour while heading for the kitchen. Although the house looked intimidating from the outside, the inside was just the opposite. It had contemporary furnishing with a really homey feel. A feeling of peace and calm enveloped her as Tanya dragged her through Roxel's parent's home. In the kitchen was Mrs. Stapleton, a woman who was introduced as Tanya's cousin, and the housekeeper. Each woman's hands were busy preparing something. "What can I help with?" she asked.

Mrs. Stapleton asked if she could make the frosting for the cake. Baking was one of her mom's specialties and she had frosted many cakes. "Absolutely," she said as Tanya handed her an apron. There was a huge red velvet cake sitting on a stand. Pharise would use her mother's special recipe that included a little lemon and orange juice in the cream cheese frosting. The ladies laughed and talked as they hurriedly finished everything. When she finished the cake, all eyes were on her.

"Where did you learn to decorate cakes like that?" Tanya asked.

She wasn't modest, but she was proud of what her mom had taught her. "My mother baked cakes for all kinds of events and she would usually frost them. It just developed after a lot of practice."

Mrs. Stapleton chimed in, "Well it looks fantastic." They all stuck their fingers of the remnants in the icing bowl. The look on their faces told the story that the icing tasted as good as it looked. She was quite pleased.

"We're going to take everything out to the buffet table. This will allow everyone the ability to fix their own plates. They transported one dish after another out to the huge dining room that seated at least twenty. After the last dish was taken out, Mrs. Stapleton asked the housekeeper to go and let the men know that dinner was ready. Mrs. Stapleton and her husband shared cooking duties, both liked cooking and entertaining. It was her turn and she hoped all went well. Pharise was a natural beauty. She had poise and class. She didn't know why, but she was drawn to this opinionated, spunky, and in-your-face young woman who kept her son off-balanced. A knowing smile tilted the corners of her mouth into a smile. She would just sit back and watch the fireworks tonight.

Roxel was ready for a good home cooked meal. He'd been staying late at the office and grabbing a sandwich and salad when he got home. He knew that staying late was a way to wash Pharise from his mind, but it had not been effective. He continued to think of her and little things reminded him of her. The old adage, "time heals all wounds" was not working well for him. His feelings for her continue to grow even in her absence. If he could shake some sense into her, he would. He was certain that wouldn't go over too well with her, but it was an idea. He would be flying out in the morning to have the last interview with the candidate who they hoped would accept the position of plant manager. There hadn't been any more major incidents at the plant and things were getting back to normal. Things were looking better. Maybe, he should take some time and figure out what he really wanted in his personal life. He looked forward to taking back his full-time job as CEO of the company in the near future.

They had been summoned to the dining room to eat. He headed for his usual chair beside his father. He hadn't really noticed who was already in the room. He sat down and stretched his legs out in front of him under the table. He was lost in his own thoughts when she glided into the room. What was she doing here and who invited her? His eyes found his mother and he could see a hint of a smile on her face. She was up to something. He would just sit back and relax and see how this whole thing played out. It would take herculean strength to keep his libido in check. He could feel his slacks tightening in the crouch. Pharise was wearing a fitted champagne colored dress with a square neckline that hinted at her full breasts. The dress ended right above her knee and tightened around her full scrumptious behind. His mouth watered as he checked her out. He was certain his mother was watching him eyeing her, but he didn't care. His mother was devious enough to have planned this whole thing and he planned to enjoy himself. He hadn't spoken to Pharise in a couple of weeks. She had called him several times, but he hadn't answered. He had been so busy at the plant that he had missed each call. He had plenty opportunity to return the calls, but he decided against it. He didn't know if he could take any more rejection from her. He convinced himself that he wouldn't push her, but he was thinking that he needed to change his strategy. Tonight, she would get fair warning that she was now being pursued.

Pharise's eyes came up from what she was doing to meet Roxel's intense stare. "Hey, how are you doing?"

He got up from his seat to help her with the cake she was carrying to place on the buffet table. She allowed him to help her. "You didn't make this cake did you," his eyebrows bunch together in a slight frown.

"No, I just made the frosting and I iced the cake."

The cake looked like it should be entered into one of those contests. He couldn't believe she had done it. "It is a culinary masterpiece, Ms. Mallard." His face glowed with the sexiest smile. He pulled out the seat nearest him for Pharise to sit. She accepted and he pushed the chair to the table. Everyone was seated and his father said the grace. Everyone watched the exchange between him and Pharise. Now things were back to normal with everyone fixing their plates, talking, laughing and having fun. It had always been this way with his family. They were happy people who had been blessed to share their happiness with others. He stood behind Pharise as she fixed her plate. He was way closer than he should have been. His thigh was touching her behind. He wanted to see if she would inch forward to disconnect the union, she didn't.

"You look really good, Ms. Mallard". He whispered this near her ear. The soft moist breath on her neck was almost her undoing. She did everything she could to keep from dropping the plate. He inched closer where she could feel his chest on her back. It was then that she felt her panties moisten with liquid fire that he was causing. She convinced herself that she wouldn't back down to Roxel. He was trying to seduce her in a room full of people, the nerve of him. She was aware of his tactics and he was very good at his game, but she wasn't going.

She turned and looked up into his face and her breath hitched. She felt herself sway just a bit. Before he could assist her, she caught herself. If he was issuing a challenge, then she was game. "You're on, Roxel." He laughed, understanding that she had accepted his challenge. She turned around and continued to fix her plate as if his presence didn't unnerve her. This challenge would likely be the death of them both, but he was definitely ready for it. She thought she would lean forward just a bit to get things going. Her behind brushed up against his crotch and she straightened, apologizing all the while for bumping up against him.

He planned on paying her back in spades. His erection was probably the size of a small mountain by now. He planned to escape back to the table before anyone noticed. He intended to enjoy this night. All the food looked so good. For some reason his appetite was bigger than usual, he piled his plate high. He would speak to his mother later about her part in all this. Everything was delicious and they had all bragged on Pharise's frosting on the cake. He had found himself the butt of many of the jokes that night, but it was all in fun. He noticed that Pharise was really enjoying herself with his mother and sister, so it was all good. After dinner, the men put away the dishes. This was one of his families' traditions. One gender cooked and the other one cleaned. The ladies sat out on the patio and enjoyed the cool weather. They drank iced tea and glasses of wine as they relaxed after a good meal. It took about forty-five minutes before the men joined them. It was after ten and no one wanted the evening to end. They continued to talk. Tanya was the first one to leave. She shared a medical practice with a friend and she had to make rounds at the local hospital. It was amazing that she hadn't gotten married, yet. Roxel wondered what she was waiting on. He had taken a seat next to Pharise. Although they hadn't said more than ten words to each other since dinner, they were emotionally communicating with each other on a much deeper level than before. His parents bid everyone good night saying that they were too old to hang with the young folks, which was completely untrue. He and Pharise were being set up and they both knew it. Pharise was about to say good-night when he suggested a quick tour of the house of which she agreed. Roxel assisted her into getting back into her four inch stilettos that she had worn to make herself look more desirable. She leaned into him as she slid her feet into the shoes. The closeness caused his stomach to do a somersault. He could tell she was a little tired. His hand possessively went around her waist to give her support. They quietly walked in and out of each room. As her unofficial tour guide, he counted their time together as precious. They strolled the span of the house with him giving information about the artwork and the different family portraits that graced the rooms. This was an enchanting evening. He walked her to her car and his arms circled her waist. "Hey, I had a really good time. I don't know whether my mom or sister extended the invite, but I'm glad they did."

He leaned in and conquered her mouth seducing it one kiss at a time. She knew her breathing had changed. This man was intoxicating. His cologne was that familiar woodsy odor and his natural scent was driving her wild. Her hands clutched his neck pulling him closer until she could feel his erection in her middle. She wasn't afraid of him tonight or the passion that they emitted whenever they were in the same room together.

He pulled his mouth away from hers first. "Are you trying to seduce me, Ms. Mallard?"

"What if I am," she boldly declared. Their eyes locked in a heated stare down.

He simply said, "That would be my pleasure". He opened her car door and helped her get seated. He reached over to lock her seat belt in place. He gave her another passionate kiss. He closed the door and headed for the little red corvette. She drove off toward the hotel wishing that she had enough nerve to head to his place. She was getting there, but hadn't quite arrived yet. Roxel stayed pretty close as he followed her back to the Renaissance hotel. She entered the valet parking lane and left her car with the keys inside. Roxel got out of his car sauntered in her direction. When he reached her, his lips lowered to take in hers. It was an explosive kiss that only lasted a few moments, but it spoke volumes. He was staking his claim. She nodded communicating that she understood. He walked back to that little red corvette and he was gone. She was still standing in the same spot that he left her trying to figure out the magnitude of that kiss. It wasn't like she had never been kissed before. She had never been kissed so thoroughly or felt so much need in a kiss. It was at that moment that she became afraid of Roxel Stapleton. He was the one in control of this situation and he didn't even realize it.

Chapter 17

ROXEL CAUGHT THE "RED EYE" to Las Vegas to interview this candidate for the fourth time and to make him an offer. It would require him to remain in Las Vegas for at least three days to take care of the business. His family was looking at a smaller company that was in financial trouble. The company produced micro optic fibers. If everything worked out they would acquire the company within the next six months.

His mind wandered to Pharise. He wondered what she was doing. It was obvious that she made friends easily. She had overheard Pharise tell his mother that the girls were all getting together at a local restaurant tonight. His sister and Pharise had mentioned that the ladies had several lunch and dinner dates. They had even gotten some shopping in. She, Dr. Jackson, and his sister, Tanya had been hanging tough. He also wondered what she had thought of their last kiss. Saying that it was explosive was an understatement. He hadn't asked Pharise to accompany him to the benefit. It was evident that she was still uncertain. She hadn't said a mumbling word as to whether she wanted to proceed with a relationship and he believed he had given her enough space. He wouldn't make it back home until the afternoon of the benefit. He planned to spend some quality time with Pharise when he returned home. He would call her and make his intentions known.

He grabbed a cab after retrieving his luggage and headed for the Bellagio hotel on the strip. His plans were to shower, order room service, and get a good night sleep. The room was spacious and accommodating. The large king size bed reminded him of Pharise and that made him horny. He hadn't made love since the episode with him and Pharise. His body was yearning her. He pushed thoughts aside to focus on the work he had to do. After reviewing some legal documents regarding the potential acquisition, he ordered in and retired for the evening. His body was suffering from jet lag and sleep came easy.

The next three days flew by. Things had gone well with the interview. The candidate accepted the offer and would relocate to Washington within the month. They offered him a generous relocation package and a sign on bonus. However, they were not that successful with the acquisition process. The troubled company was stalling. Roxel assumed that they were looking for some type of bail out so that they could maintain the integrity of the company. Roxel knew that the help they desired would probably never come. He would wait about a week and send it the hard hitters. They would seal the deal.

He missed his scheduled flight and things did not look promising for the next flight back to Washington. There were only a couple of seats left and there were about ten people waiting for seats. If he didn't make this flight, it was likely that he would miss the benefit all together. He telephoned his mother and asked her to pick up his tuxedo from his home along with his grooming products. If he made the flight, he would have just enough time to shower and change. The flight was scheduled to leave in the next twenty minutes. He was reviewing some documents when he heard his name being called. He must have done something right in life. He landed one of two seats. He was issued a boarding pass and he boarded the plane. He was grateful for an aisle seat in first class. He leaned back in his seat and was overtaken by sleep. His dream was of the most sensual kind. Pharise was in his home sitting on his deck in a golden tee-shirt and a thong. They were playing naughty games with chocolate and fruit. He was plunging in and out of her sweet moist warm body when he heard the airline attendant announce they were preparing for landing.

It was five fifteen and the benefit would start at seven. By the time he claimed his luggage and reached his car, thirty minutes had passed. He made the forty-five minute drive to his parent's home in thirty minutes. He entered from the rear of the home. Guests had already arrived and his parents, being the perfect host, were attending to their needs. His mother turned to see him as he rushed up the back stairs, which were mostly obscure from the guests. His mother had placed his things in his old room. He dressed in record time, but it was almost seven thirty before he reached the ballroom. He kissed his mom on the cheek.

She greeted her son. "I'm glad you made it. I thought your father was going to have to stand in for you as the toast master. Roxel said, "That would have been a real hoot. His humor is so dry sometimes. You know he's not funny." His mother laughed. Roxel waved at his father who was busy "politicking" as his mother politely described. His mother adored his father. Things had not always been that way for them, according to his mother. When they were younger, there ambitions had pushed them apart. It was then that his dad decided that both of them needed to commit to working fewer hours per week and spend quality time with each other and their children. His parents had told them that they never regretted that decision. They complimented each other. They allowed the other one space to pursue the things that they enjoyed. His mom was not a sports' fan, unlike his father who was passionate about every sport. The two just learned to appreciate and respect each other. He was proud to have parents who still loved each other. It was a rarity.

Roxel mingled among his peers and co-workers. He grabbed a glass of champagne from a passing attendant. The room held about two hundred people, was packed. He eyed his sister and brother across the room conversing with some old friends. His brother, Trevor, was home. He was the marketing director for the company which allowed him to travel. He figured that traveling would keep him out of harm's way. According to Trevor, he had no intention of getting caught by a woman. He enjoyed women, but he enjoyed his freedom more. There were a number of people who were de-stressing on the dance floor. Everyone looked like they were having a good time. He was glad to see that John wasn't wasting anytime with the good doctor. She was stunning in a black and white fitted gown. She was the envy of most of the women there.

The workers deserved a retreat from the daily grind. The accidents had placed a shadow on the image of the company. Roxel could feel the champagne going straight to his head. *I should have eaten something first, he thought.* It was then that he saw her. One of the board members who was known to be a ladies' man was hovering over her. He was one of those GQ types that looked like he doubled for a fashion model. Every time he saw her, something tugged at his heart. He had never been jealous of a woman before. It was a foreign feeling to a man that had his pick of good looking women. Still, he was overcome with an emotion that he couldn't quite put a name to it.

She wore a silver gown that sparkled with silver, gold, and black gems that were sewn on. The plunging back of the gown gave an erotic visual of the indention of her hips. One side of the fashion masterpiece had a split that was trimmed in a silver and gold lace like material. Her thick breast swelled over the top of the rounded neck. Her hair was pulled up to the crown of her head and twisted in some exquisite knot. It was held together by a long chop stick looking ornament. Wavy curls escaped from the twisted knot on her head and cascaded around her face, which was highlighted with bronze and gold make up. It was a face that he loved. *He would not spend too much time trying to figure out the when, the how, or the why. Only time would tell what would be in their future.* Pharise had transformed into a sensual vixen and he was caught up in her allure. He believed that because of an unseen emotional connection, they could sense the other's presence. He was about to put his belief to a test. He stood motionless in the same spot for less than a minute sipping his drink when her head intuitively turned to meet his glare. There, that proved what he believed all along. They were connected by something greater than the both of them. He held her gaze a few moments more so that she would be clear of his intentions. She excused herself from the man who had been extremely attentive to her moments earlier. She turned completely in his direction and he had her undivided attention. Unbeknown to him, his parents watched this exchange as they stood near the open bar. His feet moved in her direction and she was transfixed and rendered immobile. As his approaching presence became bigger than life, she lifted her head to look into his face. "I thought you weren't going to make it. Your mother and sister invited me, since you didn't mention it. I don't want you to feel obligated to hang out with me. I'm sure your date wouldn't like that." Roxel looked better than any man should or could. He was the perfect composite of masculinity in its finest. She could honestly admit that this brother was wearing the silk black tailored tuxedo that hung on him like it was specifically designed with him in mind. He chose to wear a crisp monogrammed white shirt that buttoned at the collar and required no tie. A bronze cummerbund pulled the ensemble together. He wore Italian leather black slip on shoes that boasted of a spit-shine. He took dressing to a different level. If she was looking all giddy and stupid, then so be it. He was not the flavor of the month. He was, hands down, the flavor of a lifetime and he was looking at her like he wanted to swallow her whole. At this moment, the word "no" was not in her vocabulary. Tomorrow might be a different story.

She was searching for some answers. Roxel would let her squirm a little. He pushed a wayward curl off her face and looped it behind her ear. "You're enchanting this evening, Pharise." She smiled up at him and that did it for him.

Pharise looked at Roxel with admiration.

"I didn't think I was going to make it in time, either." He explained about missing his plane and there being only two open seats on the next flight. He didn't have to ask if she missed him, it was written on her face.

Roxel didn't consider himself to be a real dancer, but he was dying to be close to her. He missed her and there was no denying it. She had been on his mind and had invaded his dreams every night. She was irritating sometimes and bull-headed other times, but she was his correct change. There was no one else that he would rather spend time with to his way of thinking. He leaned over and whispered in her ear, allowing the moisture from his breath to penetrate deep within her pores. She felt the vibration from his words on the sensitive spot on her neck. "Come on and dance with me," he said.

Her mouth opened and then closed. She hadn't danced in years. Usually when she went to events, she would just hang around the perimeter of the room and network a little. It wouldn't take long for her to get bored with the scene. She didn't drink alcohol and rarely danced. She would make an exception to dancing this one time.

He took her hand in his larger one and ushered her to the area designated for dancing. He pulled her so close to him that there was no space between the two. Her soft body melted in to his. As he held her in a tight embrace, he sang James Ingram's song, "One in A Million." She couldn't recall if this had ever been one of her favorites, but this man was doing something that the other men in her life failed to do. He was wooing her and he was taking his own sweet time doing so. As much as she regretted it, she had to admit that he wasn't a bad singer at all. His smooth melodious voice was stirring something down in the marrow of her bones. When he pulled her to the dance floor, he mentioned that he wasn't a great dancer. Well, he lied. Initially, she tried to keep up with his moves, but failed miserably. When she allowed her body to lean into his and follow his moves, they were able to glide across the floor like they had danced together a million times. She would imagine that it looked pretty erotic to on-lookers. He held her hips as their bodies moved as one while at other times his hands glided freely up and down her body as he held her in place as he twisted, turned, bent, and leaned her. They were in sync, perfect harmony. She couldn't remember having this much fun before or engaging in movements on the dance floor that belonged in the bedroom. Her panties had to be saturated from her arousal. Roxel didn't compare to anyone in her past. In fact, Spencer rarely ever did anything that didn't involve him being the center of attention. He would always find a reason to disagree with something she had said or done. She had limited accompanying him to social gatherings after his temper worsened. No matter what she did, their evenings always ended when him being mad at her, but that wouldn't stop him from wanting to have sex. She wondered if he didn't know that being mad and having sex were polar opposites. Anyway, she had made up her mind that she wasn't going to fight with him on everything. She had moved on mentally and emotionally long before she left him. She hated herself for mentally comparing the other men in her life to Roxel, but she couldn't stop it. Roxel was not a selfish man. He had proven this even when she was injured. He was always trying to make sure that she was okay and that she had what she needed. She guessed that this was one of the reasons she was staring up at him like he hung the moon. This would be a night to remember.

After the dance of a lifetime, Roxel received a phone call from the plant. It seemed that the culprits were at it again. He left the ballroom to take the call. Most of the management team were in attendance and all of them were dressed to the nine's. This seemed to be the social event of the year. Only a skeleton crew was working tonight in order to give everyone a reprieve so that they could attend. There were plenty of clingy women and men who had one too many drinks. She hadn't seen the quality manager tonight. She wasn't an easy person to miss. Pharise assumed that she would have been close on Roxel's heels. She wasn't complaining about the lack of competition. She was just wondering.

The evening lengthened until early morning. Some of the attendees were beginning to leave and Roxel hadn't made it back, yet. The men there were overly friendly and she had her share of male advances for the evening. She didn't want to admit it, but there was only one man who was on her mind. She hoped that there wasn't another accident at the facility. She hated to leave without saying good night to Roxel. She hoped their evening wouldn't have to end so early. If he asked tonight for her to join him at his home, her answer would "yes". She was mentally preparing herself for whatever this thing was between the two of them. She was headed toward the coat check to pick-up her wrap. Although it was spring, the nights were chilly in Washington. She was intercepted by Roxel's father. "Are you leaving so soon?"

"Well, it's getting a little late and most of the guests are leaving or have already left." She wouldn't admit that she had been stalling to find out if Roxel was coming back.

His father explained, "Roxel asked me to make sure you made it home safely. He left about thirty minutes ago. There was a fire at the facility. It looks like it was contained to a small area and there was only a minimal amount of damage. Jessie had gotten wind of the perpetrators' plan and had agents positioned to apprehend the perpetrators. This time their plan may have backfired." She was a little disappointed that he left without letting her know. She knew he didn't owe her an explanation, but thought that he would have said something to her before leaving. Her disappointed look must have been obvious to Mr. Stapleton.

"He wanted to come back in to tell you that he needed to leave, but I convinced him to go ahead and leave so that he could arrive before the police arrived. I told him I would make sure that you knew of the urgency of the situation. I was on my way to tell you when some of my colleagues ambushed me. We were discussing some new business ventures and the time got away from me. I sincerely apologize. Please, don't blame Roxel. He will have my head if he finds out that I didn't let you know immediately that he had to leave. He told me he would call you a little later and wanted me to make sure you got home safely."

Pharise hoped the night would have ended differently, but realized the plant's issues took precedence, tonight. "Oh, I drove tonight. It's no problem. I really had a good time. Tell Mrs. Stapleton that everything was wonderful and she outdid herself."

"I will let her know. She was helping the caterers earlier and is probably in the kitchen as we speak. My wife and I were discussing you earlier."

She looked bewildered, not understanding what he was talking about. "Why were you discussing me?" Pharise understood why Roxel was so good looking and charming. He was a chip off the old block. She had noticed that quite a few of the ladies had eyes for the older Stapleton. He seemed to take it all in stride.

"We both think that you are absolutely stunning tonight. It seems that our son is a bit taken with you. We thought that this was a bit funny, since he is a declared bachelor. In fact both of my sons have admitted that single life works for them. Their mother and I know that both of them are lying. It's the same lie I told myself more than forty years ago until their mother caught my eye. I made it my business to make sure that I convinced her that I was the only man on earth that was suitable for her. She laughed in my face, but you see that my mission was successful." He was smiling as he relived fond memories.

"Thank you both for those kind words, but Roxel and I are just friends. I really like him. I have way too much baggage in my life to get involved." She didn't know who she was trying to convince, Roxel's dad or herself.

"Pharise I hate to tell you, but you are already involved. Consider yourself warned. My son is quite fond of you. And take my word for it that is a rarity. Don't you agree that he's a pretty good catch?" His eyes twinkled with amusement.

"Yes, I agree Mr. Stapleton". He escorted her to the coat check to get her wrap and then walked her outside as the valet returned with her rental. Mr. Stapleton opened the door for her and waited until she secured her seat belt before closing the driver's door. As she drove out of the estate, she could see Roxel's father rooted in the same spot waiting for her to safely leave the property.

Chapter 18

PHARISE ARRIVED BACK at her hotel around one thirty, showered and dressed for bed. She clicked on the television and watched the news caption. The fire at the facility had been contained to a storage room that contained recycled composite pieces for the prosthetics. They were interviewing Roxel. He elaborated on the rash of staged incidents at the plant. They arrested two men tonight who were believed to have been responsible for at some of the incidents. He eluded that these men were not the ring leaders. She saw Jessie and two of the agents in the background. They were very efficient. There was no doubt that they would find all those who were involved. She noticed her breathing had changed and she was getting worked up again. She closed her eyes to focus on breathing in and out and thinking of something non-threatening when she heard a knock on her door. She opened the door weakly after recognizing Roxel through the peep hole. She opened the door and gave a faint greeting before returning to the bed and collapsing.

Roxel caught her before she hit the bed. If he hadn't she would have hit her head on the railings. She was somewhere between sleep and disoriented. He lay in her bed cradling her in his arms. It didn't take her long to come to herself.

"I'm sorry. I'm not sure what triggered that panic attack. I was watching the news about the fire at the plant and I was having an episode before I knew it."

"Tell me what usually triggers your panic attacks." His voice was soft and comforting.

"They come when I'm really stressed about something and sometimes there's no rhyme or reason to them." Roxel believed he knew what precipitated her anxiety attacks. He was no psychiatrist, but he was pretty observant. Usually, her attacks came after stressful events, like the car wreck. It was as if her mind and body went on auto pilot during periods of "fight or flight." He didn't have a remedy for her problems. Pharise needed to learn how to relax. She was going through an emotional catharsis. She leaned into Roxel and talked some more. "Am I talking your ear off?" She was amazed that he was really hearing her. She turned to look in his eyes. What she saw should have frightened her, but it didn't. His eyes told her a story and she knew that he wanted her to see past all of her hang ups and issues.

He wanted her know that he was in it for the long haul. He was not into playing games with women. There had never been a need to confess his love to a woman before. He didn't think that this was the right time now, but it wouldn't be long. "No baby, you're fine." He enjoyed listening to her. She enjoyed her family and friends and was loyal to a fault. Her life was intricately connected to church. Her mother, who she greatly admired and loved, was an educator and her best friend. Things were difficult for her after the death of her mother. She had been going through the motions in her life for the past two years. She admitted that she wanted to move past her grief and capitalize on the goodness that life offered. He was awed by her strength and resilience and he knew that this was the woman for him. Her softness oozed into his flesh and he battled the need to make love to her right at this moment. They laughed and talked over into the morning. When the sun rose a couple of hours later, it found them intertwined in each other's embrace. Roxel never bothered to undress.

He felt the sun on his face and attempted to get out of bed. Pharise had wrapped her leg around him. He wanted to get out of this "zoot suit" and get more comfortable.

"Where are you going? You're not leaving are you?" Pharise was trying not to sound needy.

"Are you putting me out?" Roxel said with just a hint of humor.

"No, I don't want you to leave. I was enjoying your company. I thought we could spend the day together." she had made up her mind, no more road blocks.

"Doing what?" Roxel's hand caressed her backside, moving up and down her legs. He positioned her body so that they were facing each other. He loved her taste and his mouth found its first target, her neck. "What happened to the marks that were on your neck," he asked while nibbling and sucking on her neck. He sucked harder as she moved under him. "What are you going to say about who put these marks on your neck?"

Her brain was so foggy. She understood the question, but didn't know how to respond with him branding her and then allowing his warm tongue to chart a path from under her ear, down her neck, and to her breasts. His hands were kneading her muscles making her muscles feel like jelly. His mouth moved back up to the hollow point of her neck and lingered. He was working the inside of her thighs inching his way to the moistened area that needed his attention. She felt the long gown being lifted above her hips as his mouth travelled lower. "Tell me what's on your mind, baby."

Surely, he must be crazy if he expected her to answer him. The only sounds that were coming from her were moans and groans of pleasure. "Oh, I think you're driving me crazy." The words came out in small gasps. The sound of bodies sliding on the sheets spurred her on. His wet lips devoured her belly button as he simulated making love as his tongue thrust in and out. She felt her bottom coming up off the bed of its own volition. Her body had a mind of its own and was reacting to every touch. This was pure torture, pure heaven.

Roxel thought she was perfect. Her taste was ingrained in his brain and on his lips. He was pressed with an urgency to love her and mate with her. This was something that he had never experienced before. She was uninhibited, a free spirit. Her response to him was unparalleled. His lips came up to devour hers as he slipped a finger deep in her core. Her flesh seized his finger tightly causing him to almost come out of his skin. He teased and taunted her clitoris daring her to release the honey that he was waiting to drink. She had been rationing out little pieces of herself since they met, but he planned that tonight that would end.

Pharise was enjoying this delicious attention. She was on fire. His hands seemed to be everywhere at one time. She couldn't escape this passion if she wanted. She knew this was a losing battle. It was at this point she gave into her emotions to allow her body to have what it craved. She leaned into his hand to accept everything that he was giving her. Her feet arched and her toes curled as she felt a stirring that began in her feet and moved up her legs. Her body seemed to convulse in a pleasurable way. Roxel held her in place to make sure she enjoyed the sensations that had taken control of her body. She tightened her legs to prompt Roxel to move his hand, but he wasn't having it. She heard herself scream and he captured her mouth to receive the passion that escaped from her mouth. She wanted to hold on to this feeling forever. Roxel said, "Just relax and enjoy. Don't hold back. Ride the waves."

And, Pharise did.

Roxel clearly wouldn't accept anything less than her total surrender. When he felt the shudders cease, he mounted her wet body. He entered her slick core in one thrust. She was still extremely tight. His breath caught in his chest. "When was the last time, baby, you made love before us?"

She knew exactly why he asked the question. More than anything she wanted to keep the lines of communication open. "It's been a while, more than a year and a half ago." She thought about the difference in Roxel and Spencer. Spencer was always concerned about his release. Whenever he initiated foreplay it was rough and rushed. She rarely enjoyed it. After a while, their lovemaking became more and more sporadic. She had suspected that Spencer was seeing someone else, but never had any evidence that this was true. It didn't really matter. Spencer never did love her, although he said that he did on many occasions. She never felt loved or cherished the way she should have and deserved. Spencer enjoyed that she was domesticated, cooked, cleaned, and made sure he looked presentable. She realized after a while, that she was doing most of the giving and he was doing most of the receiving.

He held his position while she answered his question. He continued to claim her mouth and neck enjoying the sweet salty taste. He wanted to give her a moment to adjust to him and his size. He started with short, but powerful thrusts as she continued to open her body to him like a flower opening in early morning. The more she opened to him, the more he pushed into her luscious body until he was completely inside of paradise. He settled into her and then he felt the muscles in his neck strain against his skin. His blood began to boil. He started pumping into her moist heat and she met every stroke as her muscles tightened around his engorged flesh. He felt the hair on neck rise and he pumped harder and faster. He couldn't have slowed down if he wanted to. He felt like a man possessed and then he felt it. Then, he felt her muscles contract as she locked her legs around him. A scream left her body. His body jerked and bucked against her and he released himself into her heated body. His only regret was that the condom captured his essence. He would not have minded that this woman received what he refused to give to anyone else, his seed. *This was not the time to consider this line of thinking or where the thought originated. He would deal with these thoughts another day.* At this moment, all he wanted to do was to bask in the afterglow of the most perfect lovemaking that he had ever experienced.

A ringing telephone interrupted his thoughts. "Is it yours or mine", Pharise asked. She lay spent after this phenomenal sexual experience.

"It's mine, I think." Roxel said while trying to hunt for his phone. It was Jessie on the telephone. There were new developments. They had found the leak. It was one of the managers, but more than that the union was deeply involved in the incidents as they initially believed. Jessie alluded to charges of corruption, money laundering, wire fraud, assault and even attempted murder. Jessie had information from a reliable source that there was still a "hit" scheduled for someone at the plant. Jessie had been in touch with Roxel's father and they were being protected by the feds. Jessie believed that the leak had gotten wind that the federal agents had uncovered information identifying them and had left town.

Roxel couldn't believe what he was hearing. He certainly couldn't believe that the person Jessie was identifying as the accomplice would ever be involved in something like this. He was normally able to read people pretty well, but this one was totally baffling him. The person was being detained in Houston by the local authorities. Jessie needed him to accompany him to Houston. Roxel was totally puzzled as to this person's motives. This has to be some big mistake. "I don't think that this person is capable of causing hurting anyone. What would they have to gain?" his feelings were ambivalent as to this person's guilt or innocence. He and Jessie agreed that Pharise needed to keep a low profile, especially since they didn't know who the hit was on. He was sure that this wouldn't go over well. As they spoke, he could feel Pharise withdraw from him, even though she hadn't physically moved. He couldn't divulge any information until all arrests had been made, not even to Pharise. He knew that she was listening because her breathing changed. Jessie was asking him to leave right away. They could only hold the person forty eight hours without charging them. They had tails on some of the other people involved. He clicked the phone after getting the flight information. They would be flying on a small private aircraft, which was scheduled to leave in less than two hours.

Roxel knew that their fragile relationship was in jeopardy at this moment. A sigh came from somewhere deep within. He would try his best not to lie to her, but he wasn't able to tell her the truth. A federal agent was headed to her hotel room. The plan was for her to stay at his parent's home until this thing was over. He was counting on her to trust him. This was the woman he had fallen in love with in spite of his efforts not to. Before Pharise entered his life, there had been no room for a serious relationship, until now. His heart wasn't still convinced that he was husband or even good boyfriend material. He wasn't going to admit that he hadn't enjoyed his single life, but it seemed to be coming to a screeching halt. The hardest part would be to convince her of this new revelation. This wouldn't be so easy. Her history with men hadn't been all that good. He would need her to step out on faith.

Pharise hadn't figured everything out based on the conversation she had overheard, but she knew that they were getting close to catching the ring leaders. She still didn't know why she had been targeted or why Roxel was being quiet on the telephone. Apparently, he didn't trust her enough to disclose everything that was going on. That was okay. Trust took time to build and it could be destroyed within seconds. She was in way over her head with Roxel. She was afraid that this would happen. She knew he was feeling her. Their love making was passionate and unselfish. She loved him with a desperation she had never known, but had only heard about in those romance novels she read at night. She never believed that she would be involved with a real live romance hero, but she was. He was leaving no stone unturned to transform an insecure emotional damaged woman into a confident passionate person. She would readily admit that she had loved a few men in her life, but she had never been so in love with a man as she was with Roxel. Lately, she had been daydreaming about what it would be like to be his woman and his wife. This was just wishful thinking. She inhaled Roxel's scent, that same a citrus woodsy smell and good love making. The touch of his body, a whiff of his odor, and everything about this man turned her on. She knew it was time to cut her losses and go home to Memphis, to reality. Right now, she was biding her time. She would never regret this period of her life. It truly had been cathartic and had allowed her to heal emotionally. Roxel Stapleton would always own a piece of her heart.

"Pharise, sweetheart, I know you're not asleep. You haven't been asleep for some time." He was right. She'd been listening to his conversation to Jessie, but he was sure she hadn't heard most of it. Her glassy eyes opened and his lips took hers with a possessiveness that was totally out of character for him. "Good morning." She stretched and yawned, leaning into me like a cat covering her prey.

"Hello to you, too. What's going on? Her eyelids lowered to half staff. What are we doing today?" She knew that something was up and hoped that he volunteered information surrounding all this secrecy. Their eyes met and she saw a hope that she had not imagined this connection between them. He pulled her naked body flush against his. Her were nipples hard and straining against his chest. She snuggled closer, but knew the hour of reckoning was near and she looked at the face she had grown to love. There was something else happening in that head of his at this moment that was shielded when he closed his eyes and exhaled.

Roxel gauged his words. "In a few minutes a special agent will escort you to my parents' home for a few days. You will be under the protection of the federal government. That was Jessie on the phone. They have knowledge that a "hit" is planned on someone in the family or close to our family. Based on the previous conversation you had here at the hotel with the unidentified caller and the accident, they believe that you may be the intended target. It could be me or my parents or someone else at the plant. They don't know."

She knew he wasn't telling her everything and it looked like he might not be forthcoming. She would have to ask the questions if she hoped to get any answers. "Where will you be?"

"I am flying down to Houston to identify a person of interest. They believe that this individual is involved, but I don't necessarily agree."

"Who is it?"

"I'd rather not say right now. As soon as I have more information, I'll call you and let you know. Right now, that's all that I can say about it."

Her blood began a slow boil. "That's all you want to say about it and you want me to trust you. You can't even be honest with me and tell me what you know, can you." indignation and mis-trust were clouding her senses.

Roxel wanted to say more, but couldn't until he knew for sure what was going on. "Pharise, I am telling you all that I can."

Pharise got angrier by the second. "Well, that's fine." She wasn't going to be controlled by another man. She wasn't going anywhere, especially not to his parents' home. She didn't need another baby sitter. "Correct me if I'm wrong. Wasn't I the one who was able to get the information you needed and the photos that started the ball rolling. Jessie is my company's contact and I'm the one who contacted the Labor Department to get the heat taken off your company. There's no way I should be left out."

He was simply amazed that she had omitted one little thing. She was madder than mad. Pharise would have to get over it. "Pharise, your failure to appropriately report the facts was one of the things that got this ball to rolling in the first place. If you had taken the time to interview regular employees rather than those handed to you on a platter, then your report would have looked a lot different. Don't you think? And, it's not about you being left out. You are a moving target without federal protection. I take your welfare personally. You will accept the protection that is being offered to you." Both of them were fuming at this point. Roxel's jaw line had become more prominent. The grayish tint that was usually present in his hazel eyes was long gone and replaced with a reddish hue. Frowns were etched in his forehead. He was doing everything he could to keep his temper in check, but he felt that if this conversation continued that he would blow a gasket. He opened her closet door and pulled out her Louis Vuitton suitcases. He opened a drawer and dumped her belongings in there.

Pharise was yelling now. She knew security would be there soon. "Leave my things alone. You have no right to touch my clothes."

"Fine, then pack them yourself. All I know is that you have about ten minutes before the agent gets here."

Pharise told herself that she wouldn't cry. The day that had begun with promises of a budding relationship was crumbling before her eyes. Roxel had turned on her. She held her head high and snatched the things he was holding. She wasn't packing much better than he was doing. Her vision was blurred with unshed tears. "How can you be so mean to me?" Her emotions seemed to emerge into what she believed would be an eruption. This was the same man who listened to her and didn't judge her. She would never admit to loving him. As soon as this ordeal was over, she would be Memphis bound. She had enough of the drama in this town. She would treasure all of the memories from the time spent here and lock them deeply in her heart. "You are a conceited and arrogant jerk who only thinks of himself. I really thought you cared about me. I guess I'm still that naïve girl that keeps falling for the same kind of man." She thought she saw pain on his face, but it left as quickly as it came. He was standing there looking like an avenging angel. She would never be able to forget this man. She wouldn't even try, but she would learn to live without him.

"And you, my dear, are redundant. You are spoiled and inconsiderate." Roxel's words, although spoken softly, were fierce.

She was literally tearing his heart out. If anger would motivate her to accept the federal protection, then so be it. There was absolutely no way that he would be able to leave and leave her unprotected. She was the other part of him. Nobody within ear shot could tell that right now. He knew that her anger at him would also keep her from having a panic attack and that was good. As long as she was angry, she wouldn't have time to process and deal with everything going on. He had branded her as his. No matter where she was, he would find her. "Pharise, you're wrong. I care for you more deeply than you know. However, that does not change the fact that you need this protection. We could go back and forth on this all day, but we don't have time for that. We'll talk when I get back." He knew she had shut him out. She didn't respond and she looked straight through him as she packed. He hoped that she would allow her heart to see that he was doing what was in her best interest. When he looked in her face, he knew that wasn't true. She continued to place her things in the suitcases while he stood near the door anticipating the arrival of the agent. This was a woman who could get his blood boiling with anger and then with passion. He was pulled out of his reverie when he heard her say something.

"I hate this. I hate my life and I hate you."

"Stop it Pharise. We're not even going down that road. Stop second guessing your decisions and stop second guessing me," he said adamantly. She was pushing his buttons and she knew it.

She wanted him to hurt as much as she hurt. She had no right to say those hurtful things. She knew better. Well, she would have to repent because she wanted to see that pained look on his face.

Roxel knew that she was trying to get a rise out of him, but he wasn't going to give in to her little tantrum. "Okay".

"Okay. Is that all you have to say?" They were interrupted by a knock on the door. Roxel welcomed this interruption. They were probably about two minutes from killing each other.

The agent came in and introduced himself. Roxel gave him the address to his parents' home. The agent attempted to get her luggage. "I'll take her luggage," Roxel said. "Pharise, check to make sure you have everything. When we leave this room, I'll check you out of the hotel."

She didn't have the energy for another argument. She walked through the hotel room to make sure nothing was left. The agent left the room first and she followed him, while Roxel brought up the rear. As angry as they both were, she knew Roxel was looking at her hips as she walked. It was as if she could feel his eyes burning a hole through her. Well, she would just give him a little show. Let him know what he would be missing for the rest of his life. She allowed her body to move in perfect harmony while working her assets.

He heard himself laugh. She was giving him a real "floor show". He watched and enjoyed. Her sexy body was making him hot and there wasn't a thing he could do about it. He felt his erection press against his slacks. He was grateful that the pants were able to stretch to accommodate the added growth. He hoped the agent wouldn't notice. However, he knew Pharise would look and he wouldn't hide it. It was at that moment she turned to stare in his face. Her eyes lowered to his swollen crotch. She smiled believing she had a small victory and turned around. He'd concede and give her this one. He loaded the agent's car. They would ride together to his parent's home. He would then use one of their cars to head to the airport. If he'd use the sense God gave him, he would head on to the airport. He was grateful that he had packed a bag last night before coming to Pharise. It was his plan to spend some quality time with her on her turf. Normally, he was a rational and prudent person who made good decisions, but logic flew out the window where she was concerned.

Roxel rode up front with an agent and a glass divider separated them. She rode beside an agent in the back seat in silence and lost in her thoughts. This trip to Washington wasn't a failure. She had made some lifelong friends. Dr. Carolyn Trapson, Tanya, and Roxel's mother, she and Tristan had become "thick as thieves". It was as if they had known each other for years. She would stay at his parent's home until this thing blew over and then she would go back home where she belonged. Her memories of Roxel would keep her warm at night. No man would ever compare to him. When she left, there would be no regrets. She leaned her head back on the soft leather seats in the black nondescript sedan with dark tinted windows. It was a car designed for law enforcement officers. It held no plushness or luxury amenities. The agent was a good looking man. She was unable to tell his nationality. He seemed to have Hispanic, Indian, and African American features. His eyes appeared hollow and transparent. She knew that babysitting her was probably a job for a grunt, but he had not made her seem trivial. She wondered if he had a wife and family somewhere or if she would ever have a family of her own. She thought of her mother and her family. She missed them. That was the last thought she had before she was overtaken by sleep.

The car stopped and Roxel came around to her door. The tinted windows prevented him from seeing inside the car. He opened the door and was caught off guard. After all the hell she had been raising, she was asleep. He gently pulled her out the car and she snuggled up to him as he allowed her feet to meet the ground. He held her to him in a tight embrace. He felt her body trembling at his touch. Neither one had remained unscathed by this potent desire for each other and this connection that was indefinable. She had awoken at the first instance he caressed her exposed skin. "I'm still angry at you and I don't know if I will ever forgive you."

"I know that you are and you will eventually forgive me." He didn't let up on their embrace. He allowed his hands to roam freely over her face. He lowered his mouth and covered hers taking her with a pure desperation. His kiss was possessive and healing all in one. He maneuvered both pieces of luggage and still managed to have a free hand. He led her to the door and gently kissed me on my forehead. The door opened instantly and he was greeted by his parents. He said his good-byes as he rushed off to catch his plane.

$$Chapter\ 19$$

ROXEL CALLED HIS PARENTS before he arrived to their home. They were aware of the situation. There were multiple agents assigned to them as well. Although no one preferred to be in this situation, they understood the need for protection. He wasn't sure if Pharise understood the gravity of it all. He was willing for her to hate him or even possibly lose her in order to protect her. He examined the measure of his feelings for her and knew unequivocally that she was his "soul mate". There would never be another woman who fit him so perfectly. His father was now responsible for her until his return. He knew she would be a hand full. She was that kind of woman. She was opinionated, smart mouthed, and hard headed. At some point, she might attempt to escape the assigned protection. His family and the agents would be prepared. He arrived ten minutes late to the airplane landing. The plane was waiting on him. What awaited them in Houston would be no walk in the park and he needed to mentally prepare himself. He was exhausted and used this solitude and time on the plane to collect himself. He felt himself drifting off into an enchanting dream with Pharise giving him another lap dance before they ended up locked together in pure bliss.

Roxel's father was aware that he would probably get little sleep until his son returned from Houston. Pharise had been left in his care along with the responsibility of making sure that nothing happened to her. Pharise had not come willingly. She probably felt that she was an intrusion in their lives and a bother. She was neither. She had no idea that his son was deeply in love with her. If she had, he believed that her spirit would be calmer. His wife had shown her to her room and helped her get settled in. As far as he knew, his son had never been in love with anyone before. It looked as if Roxel's running days were almost over. Whatever their issues, he was certain that with a foundation of love and trust that they could overcome them or learn to deal with them. The cup of coffee he had been nursing had gotten cool while he waited for the woman he adored to return to the kitchen where she had left him. He sighed and wondered what the next few days would hold as he got up to refresh his cup.

Tristan could recognize a woman in love anywhere. Pharise was in love with her son. She had hoped that he would find someone in his life to complete him and she believed that Pharise was that woman. He was happier when she was around and she was able to make his rough edges seem a little smoother. She was also a woman who was angry with him. She felt that he was trying to control her and failed to consider her feelings. She was wrong; women often were in that respect. She would do what she could to help Pharise find her way. This young woman had endured more than her share of losses in her life. She had just rounded the corner when she picked up the scent of the man who she had pledged her life to less than fifty years ago. She still loved this man even when he was exasperating.

"How's she doing", he asked.

"She'll be fine." She was hopeful things would work out for them all.

Chapter 20

MK KNEW THINGS were going downhill fast. He hadn't planned on the federal agents tailing his men. Now, he would have to deal with the person siphoning him information at the plant and his own men. It had been a while since he had pulled a trigger, but he wasn't going down without a fight. He had transferred his assets to a family member and a foreign account. He had the slickest attorney on retainer who was successful at getting known murderers off. Today was the day for him to handle some personal business before D-day. He wouldn't regret ending the life of this incompetent excuse for a human.

He sat outside of the two-bit thug's small frame home in a rural area of town. It looked like he had used some of the money that he'd paid him to upgrade his standard of living. The man lived alone. That was a good thing. He had never left a witness alive and no one should have to die needlessly because of this man's stupidity. This man had been warned numerous times not to get caught. The word on the street was that he was spending large sums of money all over town. No one does that unless they want to be caught. He had been sitting in the thug's home for more than an hour waiting. A rental with bogus license plates was parked around the corner.

The sound of keys in the door alerted him and he positioned himself in the small kitchen. He would allow the thug to get comfortable. Where he stood afforded him a clear view of everything. Frist walked in and threw his keys on a ledge and then walked in the kitchen to grab a beer out of the refrigerator. His next stop was in the bathroom. The predictability of this man allowed him to obtain a good position. Only cowards shot people in the back. He wanted to look in his sorry eyes the very instant he recognized that his number was up. Although his neighbors didn't live close, the silencer would muffle the sound. Frist turned around and looked into the

119

face of death. Two shots ended the life of this man who probably cost him his own freedom. Frist's eyes remained open as blood pooled around his head. He wouldn't get another opportunity to botch an assignment. He had ordered two more hits, one on the union president and the other on an informant being held in a Houston jail. Competent people were hired to handle both of them. There was one more personal job to do. Roxel Stapleton wouldn't live to see his next birthday.

Jessie and the other investigative officers interrogated Janice, the quality manager. As he stood behind a two-way mirror, Roxel couldn't believe that she hated him so much. She had been the one giving information to the attackers. She had, yet, to divulge a name. Janice seemed cool and confident, which was frightening. It was as if she had done this kind of thing before. She was dressed in a loud orange dress that looked like it was way too small for her. Her breast loomed over the deep v-cut neckline. He was able to take a good look at her. She wasn't a bad looking woman, but it seemed that she was living her life way too fast. The strain and stress showed on her face. He wouldn't be allowed in the actual interview room, but Jessie had arranged for him to be able to hear and see the interrogation.

"Why were you giving confidential information to this person associated with the union? We're sure you were aware of the accidents and the injuries that were sustained. Has the company done anything to you that would make you abandon your loyalty to them", Jessie asked?

"The Stapleton's' think the sun rises and sets over them. They believe they can play with people's lives, livelihood and emotions and get away with it. Well, I wanted to 'tear down their little play house.' Those people out there deserve to have their over-time. Every since Roxel came with his bright ideas on how things could be streamlined and become more efficient, the extra work has been dwindling. Then he brings in his little girlfriend who was nothing but a snoop and a spy. I'm not saying that anyone deserved to get hurt. I'm just saying that I'm not surprised that those things happened. You don't have anything on me. I'm just a woman who talks too much."

"What about your boyfriend? Where is he and what is his real name?"

"I don't know who you are referring to? I'm a single woman and you can't prove otherwise."

"You're wrong Janice. We do have something. We noticed a fifty thousand dollar deposit into your account from a closed account. It seems that the name of that account owner has been purged from the financial institution's records. We will find out who was the owner of that account. And, you will be in less of a position to negotiate your future. It seems that another union employee has been found shot to death in his home. You might remember him. His name was Frist. You never know if your name is on a list somewhere" Jessie left the room. He was certain that he had given her something to think about. He could see the frightened look on her face. That emotion had not been there before. She was a novice playing a dangerous game.

The investigation lingered way too long. It wasn't until four in the morning when they headed back to the hotel. Janice had finally given up MK's full name. His birth name was Milton Kayne, native of Baltimore Maryland. There was a lengthy history of his involvement with shady union affairs. He had stacked numerous charges up over the years. His fancy lawyers and hefty bank account kept him out of prison. Jessie informed him that the word was that a hit was still ordered on his family. Federal agents followed then at close range. He shared a suite with Jessie and wasn't allowed to go out alone or answer the door. This period of strange quietness was welcomed. There was plenty of work that needed his attention.

He had called Pharise after showering. Her phone went straight to voice mail. His next call was to his father who answered immediately. He updated him on everything that occurred at the jail and with the interrogation. He knew his dad could read him like a book and he was stalling for information on Pharise. "I tried to call her, but she didn't answer the telephone. Is she alright? Dad, would you see if Pharise will take my call?"

Before his dad responded to the question, he talked about them being under house arrest and not being able to leave without the agents. They were taking it all in stride. Pharise seemed to be less angry and was settling in according to his father. In fact, they had been having a lot of fun. Since, they couldn't go out. In the evenings, they played scrabble and taboo. Tanya and Rolland were both home until this thing was over. She's like a second daughter. She's a pistol just like your sister. They both laughed.

"Son, don't make a lot out of it if she doesn't want to talk to you. She might need a little time. She hasn't mentioned you or asked about you since you left. I assume that's not a good sign that she's over whatever was bothering her."

The seconds seemed to lengthen to hours before his father returned to the telephone. He knew Roxel wasn't going to like her answer. "She says right now she's busy and will have to get back with you."

Roxel closed his eyes wondering if things between them could be repaired. She was distancing herself from him. If he was home, he would try and talk some sense in her. He was thousands of miles away and there was nothing he could do. "What should I do, dad? I've never been here before. I feel like I'm losing her and I can't allow that to happen."

He wished that there was some way to help his son. He didn't make it a practice to get in his children's personal affairs and he had no intentions of starting. However, he felt his son's pain. "If you push her, it's likely that she'll keep running. Maybe, she will change her mind and talk to you later."

Roxel knew that was highly unlikely. She was stubborn and she had made up in her mind what she felt was in her best interest. "Just let me know if she needs anything or if she is alright."

"I will, son. Get a good night sleep. You've had a full day." They ended the call.

He'd been in Houston for five days. Each night he'd called home to check on his family and to find out how Pharise was doing. She hadn't returned any of his calls. There was no denying it, he missed her. Jessie hoped to get everything wrapped up in the next day or so. It was still the belief of the feds that regardless of how things were going, someone might try to take a member of his family out. Everyone was moving around very cautiously under their protection.

She wondered how things were going. Intentionally, she failed to answer his evening calls. His father continued to update her after he had spoken with Roxel nightly. His father didn't miss anything. He would search her face as he spoke about his son. She tried unsuccessfully to mask her feelings, but she was certain he saw right through veil she wore. Avoidance had become her mantra lately. He ignited passion within her. The panic attacks had become less frequent with less intensity. She was overwhelmed by the power that he held over her. When he was near, it was hard to refuse him anything. She had decided to leave before he returned. As soon as she received word that things were over, she would be headed home. Washington was a temporary home. It was not where she belonged. Roxel was simply infatuated with a Memphis girl. She wasn't the uptown sophisticate he was accustomed to dating. Once she left, he would quickly move on. She was certain of this.

She had fallen asleep reading and drifted into a delightful dream. She loved chocolate covered strawberries. Roxel drizzled warm chocolate onto her naked body. He took his finger and swirled the chocolate into every erogenous zone she possessed. Her moans provoked him to continue. His mouth followed the path of his fingers to devour every drop of the chocolate. His warm moist mouth felt like it was engulfing her very soul. If she allowed him to continue, she knew she would never be able to tell him to stop. Those four letters were just like the game they had played earlier, taboo. She could feel the moisture that settled between her legs dripping as he raised her hips around his shoulder to continue his assault. After the last mind-blowing orgasm, he filled her with his unprotected hardness pumping her like a mad man until he was spent. Before he offered her his seed, their eyes met and he silently asked the question. Words weren't necessary. Instead, she grabbed his buttocks holding him tight to her core until he had released everything into her. As she woke up from the dream that seemed so real, moisture collected in her panties. She realized that she would ponder the meaning of this dream for a lifetime.

Night had fallen and the air was crisp with a light breeze. The trees were bending with the weight of the wind. It would be a good night for a drive. This was probably not one of her better ideas. Without considering the consequences of leaving the safety of the Stapleton's' property, Pharise secured the seatbelt of her rental. Roxel had arranged for a driver to bring her car to his parent's home. It had been left in one of the three driveways that surrounded the home. She placed the car in neutral and allowed it to roll backwards far enough to give her room to turn around. In order not to alert his parents everything had to be done in the dark. As her head turned to make sure she had not driven in the yard, a voice startled her.

John had been relaxing in bed with a book he'd been wanting to read for some time while his wife worked on a medical presentation she was to give at a local community college in a couple of weeks. The vibrating telephone interrupted his reading. No one usually called this late. The number was unfamiliar to him. "Hello," he said to the voice at the other end of the telephone. One of the agents watching the home informed him that one of the residents was in her car and attempting to leave the property. He instinctively knew who it was.

"Would you like for me to stop her? This happens all the time when civilians are placed in protective custody. You won't believe the lengths people will go through just to get a few moments of freedom."

"No, no. I'll take care of it right away. Please don't notify your superiors about this. I assure you it won't happen again." His thoughts were on the young woman who had stolen his son's heart. It probably wasn't easy being in an unfamiliar home because some crazy person was trying to kill you. He was a father to a daughter with a similar personality. His daughter had made him an authority on patience. He explained to his wife what was said by the agent and assured her he would handle the situation. These were the same words he had uttered to the agent a few moments earlier. He quickly robed and headed downstairs and out the side door to where her car had been parked. Her silhouette could be seen in the short distance. He was able to arrive at the car unseen because Pharise was busy getting her bearings.

"Pharise, turn the car off and get out. It's okay. We feel the same way you do." He knew he had frightened her.

"Please, I don't want to cause any trouble, but I need to go out by myself and clear my head. I didn't mean to worry you and your wife. The both of you have been wonderful. This really isn't about anything anyone else has done or not done to me. I just need some air." All of this was said without turning around to acknowledge Mr. Stapleton's presence. It was true. It was not her intention to have them worrying about her. They had enough on their plate. She thought if she could drive awhile, she could get Roxel off her mind. It was probably easier said than done.

"No Pharise. Daughter, I need you to turn off the car. I'll pull it back up and park it." Those words had been said with finality. This was not up for discussion. Roxel had left her with them and she was their responsibility. He would make certain that nothing happened to her on his watch if he could help it.

He probably didn't have a clue as to what he had just said. He called her "daughter". She wasn't anyone's daughter. She was an orphan, no mother or father. They both had died and left her alone in this world to fend for herself. No longer able to hold things together, the waterworks began and she couldn't turn them off. She felt herself being lifted out the car by Roxel's father. This entire scene was her undoing and that was the last thing she remembered before hysteria won.

Pharise barely remembered what happened earlier. She was in bed. No amount of dreaming was going to make Roxel love her or place her on equal footing with him. It wasn't like her not to want to fight for him, but she knew that she wouldn't. His mother knocked softly on the door and entered with soup and crackers and lemonade. Not only did his mother not blame her for the episode earlier, she didn't judge her.

They talked and laughed into the morning until Mrs. Stapleton was talked out. She had given Pharise sage advice on life and relationships. Roxel's name was never called, but his mother indicated that she was very glad that they we were friends. We were more than friends. We were lovers.

Chapter 21

THERE HAD BEEN eleven arrests associated with the incidents at their facility. Some of the union officials were deeply involved in criminal activity. Allegory Medical wasn't the only company that was targeted. Similar events had occurred in at least three other facilities in the region. Janice was cooperating fully with the investigation. The ring leader had not been apprehended, yet. The feds believed that they were getting close. This was not how he planned to spend his summer. Jessie and he were headed down to the Federal building. There was still no word on MK's where about, but they couldn't remain in hiding under the protection of the government.

Normally, Houston was sunny and hot. Those were two things Houstonians could count on. However, today there seemed to be a storm brewing. It was a dreary day with low hanging dark clouds. And, this morning when he awakened he'd had a since of dread and foreboding. It was as if something bad would happen today. Nothing seemed out of the ordinary and there was no news of trouble anywhere. Still, a feeling of uneasiness covered him like the weight of his grandmother's quilt. Jessie seemed as calm as his usual self. The bulk of his time was spent on the telephone. Apparently, he had an informant who was giving him information. This information was shared with his boss at headquarters. Roxel was only privy to information that directly affected his company. He enjoyed Jessie's company. They had established an easy going camaraderie. Their new friendship would survive this ordeal.

He had packed last night. His plan was to fly to Vegas before returning to Washington to finish a business deal. Agents would continue to protect his family for the next few weeks or until MK was caught. However, they would be allowed to move around more freely. Last night when he spoke with his dad, he'd said that everything was fine. John Stapleton asked his son to be safe and hurry home. Roxel sensed that his father had not been forthcoming over the telephone. Whatever the reason for this, he would find out on his return.

Jessie alerted the other agents that we were heading from the room to the ground floor of the garage. The agents had a few loose ends to tie up and hoped that this case would be over soon. Whenever civilians were under federal protection, their lives were strained with little or no freedom. Initially, they would be cooperative. The longer things lingered, the less obliging they became. This always made their jobs a lot harder. He and Roxel had a lot of things in common. They had spent more than a week together. They'd discovered that they were both Ivy Leaguers, enjoyed sports, and were competitive chess players. Roxel didn't claim that he had a lot of friends, but he hoped that he and Jessie could continue their friendship past this experience that threatened Roxel and his family's life.

Jessie kept his eyes and ears open as the elevator descended down to the garage. Things were a little too quiet for him. There was something wrong. He couldn't put a finger on it, but his sixth sense always kicked in when danger was lurking.

"Don't move Roxel." Jessie shielded him with his body as he assessed his surroundings. The agents should have met them down on the garage floor. They were nowhere in sight. They heard an exchange of gunfire in the distance. They left the escalator and stayed close to the ground as they inched along a wall. Jessie's vision was partially blocked by parked cars.

"Just tell me what you need me to do," Roxel said. He knew Jessie wanted to find out what was happening to the other agents.

"I'm not leaving you here alone. Stay close behind me. I am going to try and get closer to my car." Jessie's car was about twenty feet away. It was out in the open and there was nothing near that would serve as a shield for them. Jessie had his weapon pulled. The gun shots were getting closer to them.

"Roxel, we're going to have to make a run for it."

"I'll move when you move. Don't worry about me. I'll keep up."

On the count of three, they made a run for the car. Gun shots stopped them short of their target. A figure dressed in all black appeared out of no way firing an automatic gun. Jessie fired back. Before they could move any further, they were surrounded by the enemy. Jessie kept his back to a concrete medium and never stopped firing his weapon. The last thing Roxel remembered was a bright flash of light in his face. Everything became a blur after that.

Roxel thought that he had died. He continued to hear gunshots, but they seemed further away. He heard people talking, although he couldn't understand what they were saying. He felt himself being lifted into an automobile. The sound of screeching sound of tires lulled him to a faraway place. And then, there was nothing.

They had been ambushed. There was no other way Jessie could explain it. The other agents had been busy holding off the assailants when they came out of the elevator. He was knocked to the ground by a three hundred pound agent who was protecting him from enemy fire. Roxel had a flesh wound that grazed his left shoulder. They were going to a safe house to patch him up. A doctor would meet them there. In the parking garage, they had left two wounded agents and six dead attackers. MK was one of the four perpetrators that were arrested on the scene. Jessie was on the telephone with his supervisor giving him a rundown of the events. He had no doubt that they would find out who leaked the information as to where they were staying.

The television program was cut in by a breaking story. There had been a gun fight with federal agents and union personnel with Washington, DC ties. There were six confirmed dead, four people were injured and there were multiple arrests made. One could have heard a pin fall in the Stapleton's family room. No one moved or spoke during the story. "John, find out what's going on," Mrs. Stapleton said. Her eyes were wet with unshed tears and her voice trembled. She called Roxel's phone numerous times, but there was no answer. Mr. Stapleton remained calm on the outside. His eyes hinted at his internal feelings of fear of the unknown. He dialed Jessie's number and received no answer. He called the agent in charge of protecting them.

"What is going on? We just saw a "breaking news story" that involved federal agents down in Houston. Was Roxel and Jessie involved?"

The agent didn't have much information. He shared what he knew. There was no information or whether either one was hurt. "They were involved in the shoot-out. There's been no word yet as to who was hurt. I've been on the telephone the last few minutes trying to get more information. I've put a call in to my superior and I should get a call back any minute." The agent hung up to keep his telephone line clear.

Roxel's brother was the talkative one in the family. He was talking non-stop in a nervous way. His mother just sort of stared in space and the bowed her head and mumbled a few words of prayer. Her faith had been the glue that held her family together. It was this same faith that awarded Pharise a peace she didn't quite understand. Tanya simply refused to believe that anything bad would or could happen to her brothers. This whole thing felt like an out-of-body experience for Pharise. She watched the movement of the mouths of the news persons, but no sound seemed to come out. "God please, don't let Roxel be hurt" she said in a muffled voice, but it was heard by everyone in the room. No one looked at her as if she had said anything wrong. What she didn't realize and they didn't utter was that she belonged in that room just as much as they did. She meant a lot to Roxel. "When will someone call to let us know something," she said.

Roxel's father spoke first. "I've got calls in to everyone I know, including the governor. We should know something soon." His family was the most important thing in his life aside from God. He knew he didn't have the strength to endure life if something happened to any of his children. He had always been a hands-on dad. He changed diapers, fed, and stayed up late for sick duty. He made certain that he attended PTA meetings, helped with homework and projects, and was their biggest cheerleader for whatever they participated in at school. It was highly likely that he'd made some bad decisions and choices concerning his children. Sometimes, it could be said that he was too strict and rigid. In life, one seldom got the opportunity to do things over. Experiences like this helped to prioritize one's life.

The news alert continued to loop on all of the local channels and there was no word from Roxel. The family engaged in a light conversation, praying that they would receive word soon. The doorbell and the telephone rang simultaneously. Mr. Stapleton answered the door and Rolland answered the telephone. The governor's aid was on the phone. Roxel was doing fine. A bullet had grazed him and he had gotten roughed up by an agent, otherwise he was good. Jessie was doing okay as well. Mr. Stapleton received basically the same information from the assigned agent. They would need to debrief before leaving Houston and heading home. The Stapleton's home went up in a shout with them laughing and crying at the same time. This good news was welcomed. A shroud of despair was lifted off them like a storm cloud that had moved on to its next destination. Pharise joined in the celebration thanking God that Roxel was not injured. She was able to bask in the occasion and gladly accepted the unseen connection to his family. It was likely that it would be short-lived. There was no sense worrying about that now. It was a time to rejoice.

Roxel and Jessie returned to the hotel room. The fierce cloud that once enveloped them had evaporated. A sense of normality to their life would be a welcomed friend. His mind constantly re-played his time with Pharise and their conversations. He was definitely homesick. Home was not a place; it was a state of being. Pharise was his home. It was a given that she might not see things quite the same way. Recently, he'd acquired a taste for dealing with difficult things and Pharise topped the list. There was no way he would be defeated. She would be the greatest challenge of his existence.

His thoughts were interrupting by his friend, Jessie, saying something to him. "What are you going to do once you get home? Your family has been told that you are doing fine and that you are expected to return home soon. I know you're glad that this foolishness is over. Who would have ever thought that the quality manager was knee deep in this mess? I certainly wouldn't have connected it initially." Jessie was laughing. "Man, you're definitely a ladies' man. You're going to have to watch that mojo you're putting down with the women. Janice described you as an arrogant women's magnet. Given half the chance she would have done something crazy to Pharise. She believed that you two are an item." Jessie searched Roxel's face for a reaction, but couldn't quite figure out whether he was affected by what was said. "It's sad that she fell for a guy like MK who was both a low life thug and a pathological criminal. She'll get some time to consider the consequences of her actions."

Roxel considered what had gone wrong in that young woman's life that would drive her to hook up with that pathetic parasite that had ultimately stolen all of Janice's hopes and aspirations and given her a life that would include existing in a four-by-four cell. He, also, wondered how his miniscule interactions with her had precipitated such a hatred for him and the company. People never seemed to amaze him. It would be reaching to say that his attitude was cynical, but he had learned through experience that some people failed to take advantage of life's blessings. They would rather focus on what they didn't have and missed opportunities. This would never be him. Yea, Janice was a real piece of work. Roxel would have never thought in a million years that she would pull a stunt like she did. "Unless she finds herself a real good attorney, she's going to have a rough time. I'm going to contact our attorneys when I return home. They may be able to offer some help."

Jessie asked how he and Pharise were doing. Roxel answered as honestly as he knew how. "Some days, it appears we're making real progress. The next thing I know one of us or both of us sabotages our fragile connection. The one thing that I'm certain of and that is that whatever "it" is, it's both powerful and all consuming. We are powerless to control it. I just need to get home to find out where I stand with her." His goal was to win her heart. Roxel said he was in for the long haul. Pharise would need to get used to it. Roxel's statement was made with all the conviction that was innately embedded in him. He knew his new friend understood what he was saying when he looked into his glassed gray eyes. Roxel knew that as long as breath was in one's body, there was always an opportunity to love.

The private airplane landed at three thirty in the morning, he was the only civilian among a host of federal personnel. He'd give his eye tooth for a hot shower and his firm bed. They all had been awake for more than twenty hours. The hot cups of coffee were ineffective in keeping him alert. He was way overdue for some serious sleep. He drifting off to sleep and was awakened by the screeching tires of the plane hitting the tarmac. He was home and was glad things had come to an end. The efforts of the involved union members and quality manager had resulted in tragedy and death. If things had not ended, there was no telling how many others they would have hurt at the plant.

They were handed their luggage as they deplaned to a fleet of waiting black sedans with darkly tinted windows. Jessie ushered him to the first car in line.

"Where to, Roxel," he asked?

Although he would have loved to have gone to his own house, he needed to see Pharise more. "Take me to my parent's home. I've got some unfinished business there. They rode in silence. Each lost in their thinking.

His gaze was fixed on the darkness on the other side of the darkly tinted windows. Twenty minutes later the sedan pulled onto the private drive leading to his childhood home. He and Jessie said their good-byes and shook on it. There was no doubt that this friendship would last for decades. Before the car stopped good, Roxel was out and opening the massive front door with his personal key. All of the Stapleton children had access to the property. His father had made it perfectly clear that this was the family home and they were always welcome.

The house was an eerie quiet, but he pushed the foreign feeling to the back of his mind. He rushed up the antique spiral stairs that was accented by oak hardwood flooring. As children, they had loved sliding down the stairs against their parents' wishes. Their bouts with the stairs had resulted in a siblings' broken arm and lots of punishment. It still had not deterred them from sliding down the railing at break-neck speed. The thoughts of a happy childhood occupied his thoughts briefly as he took the stairs two-by-two. There was a chance that he would wake his father. His breathing was ragged as if he had run a marathon. He knocked gently at first and when he received no response, he knocked louder. He knew without opening the door that she was not there. His heart pumped hard in his chest as fear replaced dread. He touched the golden doorknob and it felt like a hot poker. Believing without seeing was not good enough for him and he opened the door to find an empty room.

His pity party was interrupted by his father. He hadn't even heard him come behind him. "She left about three hours ago. She didn't even notice that I was watching her as she rushed to leave. It was obvious that she had been crying. Her face was a mess. I didn't try to stop her. I didn't see any use in that. She would have left anyway. If I know you like I believe I do, then there's no place on this earth that she can hide." An emptiness that he had never known consumed him. "She's gone." Those two words spoke volume and they seemed so final. She had left without an explanation. Men didn't cry. He continued to chant those words as unshed tears hung in his eyes, which blurred his line of vision rendering him incapable of seeing a sealed letter lying lifeless on the bed. More than anything, he didn't want his father to see the tears that burned his face, but it was useless to avoid. Using his sleeve, he pushed away the remnant of disappointment that had moistened his face and noticed the letter. His dad touched his back in a gesture of comfort and then headed back down the hallway. "I'll call you tomorrow, dad. Tell mom I love her and that I'm fine," he said in a raspy voice that was barely audible. His dad turned to acknowledge what Roxel said and nodded. He then retreated back to his wife who loved him. He wondered if he would be able to have what his parents had. He slipped the letter in his pocket and walked back down the stairs much slower than he had walked up them. He closed the front door and entered his car, which was still parked in the driveway.

Roxel knew how to play fair, but he wouldn't. No, not today. He retrieved his phone and used the speed dial function to call he'd someone who could help him find Pharise.

"Jessie, I need a favor."

Jessie looked at his alarm clock. His body had just drifted off to sleep after having been sleepless throughout most of the last assignment. The voice on the other end of the phone was a familiar one, but one that shouldn't be waking him from his dreamless sleep.

"Why are you calling me at this God awful hour? Shouldn't you been cozying up to your woman by now?" Jessie's mind refused to erase the fog that prevented him from fully waking. His eyes remained closed hoping that the voice on the other end of the phone would go away.

"Look man, I'm in a bad way and I need your help."

Jessie's eyes sprung open as he mentally processed the desperation he heard in Roxel's voice. "Go ahead, what is it?"

Roxel knew that what he needed to ask would probably violate some ethical or legal mandate, but he would ask anyway. If this was the only way to find her, then he would do whatever that was necessary. "I need you to find Pharise. She left my parents' home hours ago without a word and I don't have a clue where she's gone. Jessie, I need to find her."

Jessie heard what Roxel was saying loud and clear. It was what he didn't say that was even clearer. Roxel gave him the personal information that he had on Pharise, including a credit card receipt that she had left in his SUV. If he'd been a thief, she had left enough information around that would allow him to steal her identity. He didn't want to take anything from her. He loved her with all of his being. She was running and he intended to find her. He had never cared this much for any other woman in his life. This was a first for him.

Jessie broke into his thoughts. "I'll get back with you within the hour. Hold tight and take a chill pill. We'll find her. I doubt if she's left the city. Is she worth me putting my job in jeopardy?"

"Yea, she's my life. No matter what happens. I'll repay you if anything goes down with your gig and I will compensate you for all the trouble."

"No need to do that. I just wanted to know if she was worth it." Jessie ended the call with Roxel and made a call to one of his sources. He grudgingly left the comfort of his bed to go into his office. He would be able to locate Pharise in a few minutes if she had used any of her personal information." He was glad to help his friend.

An hour later, Roxel was driving back to the hotel where Pharise had originally stayed after receiving a call back from Jessie. She had booked a flight out for the next day at four in the afternoon to Miami. A gift had been given to him. It was a small one, but he was glad to receive it.

Chapter 22

PHARISE COULDN'T STOP CRYING since she left the Stapleton's home. She was grateful to be able to check back in her same room at the hotel. Her heart was broken, but leaving had been for the best for all involved. It was time to get on with a life without Roxel. She wondered if he had made it home safely and how he was doing physically and emotionally. She was sipping on a cup of chamomile tea to help calm her. It always seemed to help her in the past, but its effect was minimal today. She hadn't bothered to unpack. She would be on a plane leaving Washington tomorrow.

She nearly spilled the hot tea on her when she heard a knock on her door. She looked through the peephole and was astonished at the person on the other side. Internally, she had hoped that it was Roxel. "How did you find out where I was and what do you want?" she said stiffly.

"I needed to speak to you about something and I have some documents that were delivered to my home for you."

Pharise opened the door for Spencer Maxwell reluctantly. The man was still a looker, but didn't compare to Roxel. His hair was now sprinkled with a heavy dose of gray. "You have ten minutes before I put you out". You could have mailed whatever you have for me and you could have picked up the phone and called if you had something you needed to say. I thought we had said all that was needed when I left." Her eyes followed him as he sauntered over to a Queen Anne hi-back chair and took a seat. "You know you still lack manners. Don't you know that it's rude to take a seat without being asked?" this wasn't the cynical Spencer. This was more like a new and improved version of Spencer.

Spencer wondered why he had never noticed how incredibly beautiful this woman was or how merciless she kept him in check. "Pharise, all I

135

need is ten minutes. My wife is waiting for me in the lobby." It seemed she lost a little steam and unfolded her arms that were locked over her chest. She took a seat opposite him while he apologized for his tactless behavior during their relationship. He attributed his anger and hostility to being grossly over-worked and that others had been causing him to second-guess the quality of care he was giving. In addition, he admitted to feeling threatened by her ability to win others over so easily. "It was not until our relationship ended that I begin to mature". He spoke about finding a wonderful woman, who was just as spirited as Pharise. He also brought over some documents regarding her mother's life insurance policy. It seems that the unscrupulous company was being coerced into paying her and her siblings all of the money that they were initially contesting. Complaints were brought against them by other families and the federal government. Enclosed in the documents was a check that would be a nice nest egg for her family. Pharise was more than happy and certainly would forgive Spencer for this intrusion. "This was money we assumed we would never see".

It turned out that she was no longer angry with Spencer. In fact, they laughed as both acknowledged that that they hadn't been right for each other. Pharise walked him to the door and wished him and his wife well. It turned out she was expecting and Spencer was beside himself with happiness. They hugged as Pharise heard the ring of the elevator. As the embrace ended, she turned to look into the face of a very angry Roxel Stapleton.

"Who is this, Pharise? I am going to give you one minute to explain before I jump to conclusions".

One thing Pharise knew was that she would not play games with Roxel. Roxel looked like he wanted to hurt Spencer. "Roxel, this is Spencer Stapleton, the old boyfriend I told you about. He came to speak to me and bring me some documents that were delivered to him from my mother's insurance company."

Pharise was talking fast to defuse a potentially volatile situation.

The scene had appeared real questionable when he exited the elevator. He was not a violent man by any means, but seeing "his woman" in another man's arms was almost his undoing. He hands had fisted immediately and he swore that he could hear his blood roaring through his veins. However, when he looked into the eyes of the woman he loved, he knew that she was being honest. He reached for the man's hand and Spencer met him half-way. Spencer had gone on to tell him what a wonderful woman that Pharise was and how he had been the biggest jerk. Spencer excused himself quickly stating that he did not want to keep his hormonal wife waiting.

Roxel's eyes never left Pharise's face as he searched for answers to her disappearing act. She was glad he came. She was undeniably and hopelessly in love with this arrogant man, but she didn't do easy. His arm was wrapped tightly around her waist as if she intended to escape. "What are you doing here Roxel?" Her breath came out in shallow spurts. She couldn't read his expressionless face. He continued to walk her back into the hotel room and kicked the door shut.

"Did you seriously believe that I was not coming for the woman I love?" He kissed Pharise with all the tenderness he could muster. It was just another one of his ways of branding her. He went on to say, "You complete me and I wouldn't want to spend another day of my life without you as my wife." She could feel them rocking in each other's embrace as music softly played somewhere in the air that was only audible to us. "Will you be my wife, my best friend, my lover, the mother of our children and my everything?"

Tears streaked her face as the most perfect man in the world chose her. All along, she had been sabotaging her own happiness, but that would end today. "Yea, baby I will marry you as long as......" He kissed whatever smart-mouthed comeback she was going to say. She felt her feet leaving the floor as he lifted her slightly off the floor and walked backwards to the bed. He quickly got Pharise out of her clothes, almost stripping them from her willing body. He undressed himself just as quickly. He pushed her backwards toward the bed as he held her waist to brace the fall. He took her right hand and kissed it gently. When he opened his hand, in it was the largest marquis diamond surrounded by smaller baguettes that she had ever seen. He slipped it on her finger. He feathered tiny kisses all over her face before he landed on her neck. Two things happened simultaneously, he nipped the fragile flesh on her neck and he thrust into her dampened core making us one. He made the most exquisite love to her that she had ever experienced. This was just the beginning of a lifetime of happiness.

CPSIA information can be obtained at www.ICGtesting.com
Printed in the USA
LVOW10s0611030615

440888LV00002B/5/P